Love One and Hate the Other

Love One and Hate the Other

A Memoir of
Joe Billy Thompson of Sugar Hill, Alabama

Freddy Boswell

NiceFrame Publishing
Hazel Green, AL

This is a work of fiction.
The main characters of the story do not represent anyone living or dead. Nor, to my knowledge, is there a place called Sugar Hill, Alabama. It was invented for the telling of this story. If you do know of such a place, or happen to be from there, bless your heart.

There are references to public, recognizable, historical figures mentioned within the time frame of the story, such as Bear Bryant, George C. Wallace, Joe Namath, and Bo Jackson. Any reference made of them or others is as historically accurate as possible.

Printed in the United States of America
ISBN: 9798580999111

Imprint: Independently Published in cooperation with NiceFrame Publishing and Kindle Direct Publishing

Sales available through amazon.com

For Luci

A book for reading aloud with friends and family, and maybe even some college football foes.

Love One and Hate the Other

Prologue

Sportswriters and commentators have long designated the Auburn-Alabama football rivalry as the greatest rivalry in college sports. As an Alabamian, I don't dispute that declaration, but I am confident that the rivalry is about much more than just football. Instead, it is a cultural orientation, affecting every part of Alabama life, from love to vocational choices. Football opens the hearts of the people. Inside, there are amazing and intricate revelations which dominate the cultural orientations of an entire state. Thus, this is not a football tale, but a reflection on an extended and extravagant obsession, shared by millions of people. And it is usually implanted at birth.

The story is written as a fictional memoir, told through the voice and life of Joe Billy Thompson of Sugar Hill, Alabama. It is a sub-type of novel, in that while a fictional narrative, it differs strictly speaking from a novel by not following through with a consistent plot.

This story follows the life development of Joe Billy through his growing up years in small town Alabama, college life at Auburn, work life in the state capital, and eventual move to New York City, where he unexpectedly discovers the rivalry—and the cultural fabric—deeply embedded there as well. It is inescapable. On this life journey, there are a number of characters who cycle in and out of his memoir who don't necessarily advance a single or central plot, as they do in a novel, but who are important to Joe Billy's memoir which he passes down to family and friends.

This book is a compilation of an important slice of Americana that perhaps has not been as widely told as possible. As will be shown in the pages that follow, the story is colorful, dynamic, and often unpredictable. Joe Billy's choices of life-partner unavoidably intersect with the rivalry. The death of Old Man Parker is traced back to college football affection. The entryway into Joe Billy's life work was opened by an Iron Bowl classic at Auburn's Jordan-Hare Stadium. The vehicle of fictional memoir has enabled me to take liberties to describe at length and at will various possibilities and probabilities related to these cultural clashes.

Unlike other Alabama football cultural representations, such as *Rammer Jammer Yellow Hammer*, the true story of a writer who followed the Bama RV and tailgate crowd across the south during a football season, this story was invented. As no doubt all novels incorporate in some ways various snapshots and snippets of the author's life experience, similar to what Harper Lee said about some of the foundational material in *To Kill a Mockingbird*, this story stands on its own as a fictional compilation and narrative. Nonetheless, Alabamians at least will no doubt come away with both understanding nods and jogged memories, immediately turning to a friend and adding to Joe Billy's account with stories of their own.

In fact, my readers of early stages of this manuscript, and to whom I am deeply indebted for their story-line insights and supportive encouragement to pursue this creative presentation, have said on multiple occasions comments such as, "That event in Joe Billy's life about the fight in the church meeting actually happened, right?!" That question tells me that the scene is not far-fetched. The Auburn-Alabama cultural cauldron brews up so many possible concoctions, it's hard to imagine that any of them could not have happened. And Joe Billy was right in the middle of it.

There is a cultural-based theme which cycles through at various times, and shows up prominently at the end. Those from Alabama who are my age and older will not be surprised to discover it. Younger readers will shake their heads, perhaps, and ask how fictional it is. Sadly, it wasn't. I lived through it, and Joe Billy tells of it. I started writing this book in the early part of this century. I had no way of knowing that cultural wars and clashes would erupt in the year 2020 that would shine a bright light on this issue in ways we have not experienced.

The signs of cultural affinity for either Auburn or Alabama are noticed in any Walmart parking lot in Alabama. Cars owned by Auburn people are not infrequently painted with team colors. There may be a tiger tail hanging loosely and prominently from the trunk. The Bama cars are crimson, or white, or both, and often decorated with multiple school loyalty decals (and occasionally, those might number a dozen or more). Additionally, for that couple whose members of the marital duo share separate allegiances, a license plate indicating "House Divided", adorned with appropriate school logos, is not uncommon.

And just look at the attire of the folks leaving the parking lot and entering the store! Year-round—not just at football season, or game day (when it is actually worse, if that's possible)—loyalists are wearing their colors. In fact, it's not uncommon to perhaps feel out-of-place if you aren't wearing at least something to show your support. Such is daily life in the great state of Alabama.

Anyone identified as being from Alabama and who meets a stranger in another part of the country is not unfamiliar with the question, "Auburn or Alabama?" They have heard of the rivalry, and want to know which side you are on. It's a conversational starter into discerning cultural loyalty. It feels like a "Hatfield or McCoy?" question.

Joe Billy's answer was firm. The reader will discover his unexpected angst at attempting to hold on to that answer throughout his life.

And most readers will probably say that's what makes this a fictional story.

Or does it?

Part One:

War Eagle

1

The Funeral

When I looked in the casket, the first thing I noticed about Old Man Parker was the shiny, oversized Roll Tide button on his left lapel. His suit was crimson red, with white shirt, black necktie, and black belt. His shoes were patent leather black, shining like mirrors. His gray socks, with white Roll Tide lettering, clearly showed between pants legs and shoes. On his right lapel was pinned a white button with red lettering which said, "Beat Everybody." I learned later that normally when a person is placed in an open casket, only the upper half of the body is revealed for public viewing. But Parker was shown from head to toe in full, football fan attire. I was so glad they had not restricted his farewell appearance. It would have lessened the memories, and the send-off.

On one hand was a very large ring, boasting the familiar script A. Daddy told me later it was one given to each of the players on Alabama's 1965 national championship team. Old Man Parker hadn't earned it, but bought it at auction. One of the stars on the team had turned pro, made and squandered a lot of money, and had to sell his possessions to stave off the IRS. One of the prizes was this ring, and Old Man Parker had paid a pretty penny for it. While the national championship ring never left his finger, his wedding ring was noticeably absent. He claimed it was lost in a boating accident at Lake Eufaula back in 1964, and that tragedy was verified by a couple of his beer-drenched fishing buddies. However, this account was loudly and repeatedly disputed by a certain Miss Picket of Greenville, Alabama. I guess we will never know the truth. As they say, some things you just take to the grave with you.

Next to his body in the casket were various treasures. These included his diploma from the University of Alabama, class of 1932. A sampling of ticket stubs from the 342 consecutive games he had attended. His friends knew that on the morning of what would have been number 343, his wife awoke complaining of severe pain in her lower right abdomen. He had no choice but to take her to the doctor, knowing full well that if there were complications, he would miss the Tulane game which was scheduled to kick off just a few hours later. His fears were realized when about 11:30 that morning, Doc Jones performed an emergency appendectomy on Mrs. Parker. He stayed by her side while she recovered, and he pulled up a chair next to a radio for the play-by-play. Seemed horribly wrong not to be in the stadium after attending more than 30 consecutive years of games, home and away. But, after all, he declared himself to be a faithful husband. I guess he had no choice but to begin his streak over again.

Also included in the soon-to-be-buried trove, which reminded me of what I had read about the tombs of the Pharaohs in which they took their most important possessions to the after-life, was a signed game day program by a few players from the 1966 Orange Bowl game, in which Alabama beat Texas and claimed yet another national championship.

The most distinctive treasure of all was the hat he was wearing: the houndstooth fedora. It was reminiscent of the famous headgear of Paul "Bear" Bryant. According to my friend Joey, Bear Bryant was the supreme coach, of any sport of any school in the history of the world. I didn't know about that, but Joey swore by it. He was two years older than me, and he must have known. I did know that hat was the everlasting symbol of Crimson Tide superiority. There it was, snuggled onto Old Man Parker's bald, embalmed head, ready for the entombment six feet under. Though of course dead now, he was technically "inside the building", and Bear would never accede to wearing his hat inside. At the 1975 Sugar Bowl against Penn State in a place my uncle called the Super Duper Dome in New Orleans, Bear Bryant was hatless on the sidelines. A reporter asked him why he had ditched the famous and seemingly ever-present fedora, and the Bear grumbled in his gravely explanation, "Momma told me to take my hat off in the house." The fedora was the style of greatness. Bear Bryant wore one. Tom Landry of the Dallas Cowboys wore one. That should settle the conversation.

Peeking out from the brim of the fedora was a wry smile. An older mourner remarked later that it was the sort of smile that even a corpse would have when relishing memories of The Kick, from the 1985 Iron Bowl. True Bama fans always seemed to smile spontaneously whenever it was mentioned.

I was only 11 years old, and this was my first funeral. I had no choice but to assume that everyone dressed up in their Saturday best for their earthly departure. A bigger puzzle to me was why my daddy, who despised Alabama and loved everything Auburn, would even attend a public event whose central character was from the other side. Daddy later told me that at some point, you just have to lay down your grudges and do the right thing. He couldn't stay away from Old Man Parker's service just because he was a misguided Alabama fan and all. That just seemed wrong, and petty. He had known Parker for more than 50 years.

The program consisted of several things. One was what seemed to be interminable piano music. Then there was a warbly solo performance of *Amazing Grace*. Then an impassioned sermon on everlasting life by a preacher whose spit reached the second row of pews (and which was regularly brushed off by Mrs. Jenkins, who was just unfortunate enough to have chosen that spot). During the sermon, though, at one point, the preacher seemed to address Old Man Parker. He was preaching away, alternating thoughts on eternity and celebrating the great life of the great man who was now deceased, and remembering how faithful he was in the things he enjoyed, particularly a life revolving around that football team from Tuscaloosa, when suddenly the preacher looked to heaven and said, "Roll Tide, Brother Parker! Roll Tide!" Four deacons on the second row shouted in unison, "Amen, preacher! Amen!" I wondered: is this what folks do at funerals?

Finally, after what seemed like hours, in the midst of the incessant waving of hand-held funeral home fans all over the sanctuary, trying to keep the congregants cool, the time had come to march by the open casket and do something called "pay our last respects." I didn't quite understand what that meant. Sort of like when my Uncle Joe used to say that I had better eat my grits, " 'cause they will stick to your ribs." From the way he said it, I had reckoned that was a good thing.

The congregation had arisen and proceeded to file by the open casket and pay these last respects. I'm glad I was in the last third or so of the crowd that went forward so that I could observe the others and get some ideas on how to act when I got to the dead body. I had risen slowly to my feet and trudged to the front, head and eyes down, shuffling down the aisle behind my daddy.

I noticed that reactions varied. Men filed by silently, often with a brief pause and nod at the embalmed body. Some gazed and even smiled and pointed just a bit. No doubt at the Crimson Tide paraphernalia. Older ladies, for the most part, cried. A few stood in what seemed to be amazement for just a few seconds and then moved on. Others shuffled and mingled down the line, not looking too terribly afflicted. One of Old Man Parker's granddaughters had dressed up in her miniature Crimson Tide cheerleader's outfit, and she was in fine form, complete with crimson and white pompoms, and a hair ribbon of each color. She had no doubt talked her momma into letting her wear it; "Grandpa would have wanted me to!" So her momma gave in.

Some, though, threw themselves on top of the open casket and wailed loudly. Since this was my first, I had obviously never seen such an event before, and didn't know what I would do when I arrived at the moment of truth, standing front and center of the church, facing the dead body.

The weeping and wailing in the line ahead had not affected me that much. But the sight in the casket captivated me. I couldn't quit staring at Old Man Parker and his splendid and well-thought out apparel. In fact, I lingered so long that daddy tugged on my ear. "Let's go, Joe Billy!" He said it forcefully in that whispered, urgent sort of voice that meant business. Or prepare for a near-future stinging backside.

As I departed the casket sight, and tried to take in everything around me, I remembered that Daddy always said that people who weren't from Alabama just didn't understand.

They didn't understand the passion Alabamians had for college football.

2

The Daydreamer

Passion for football in the state of Alabama was defined by one play at the 1954 Cotton Bowl in Dallas, in a game between Bama and Rice University of Houston. A replay of that fateful moment was the lead film footage of every Cotton Bowl game on New Year's Day television for many years afterwards. The film shows star halfback Dicky Moegle of Rice bursting to the outside from a play that started on the Rice 5-yard line, around the Bama defense, down the sideline, headed for the end zone. No Bama player was close to catching him. But wait! He gets tackled! *How?!*

Tommy Lewis, who was not one of the 11 Tide defenders on the field on that particular play, but who was standing on the sidelines, inserted himself into the action. In other words, it didn't matter that he wasn't part of the defensive unit; in some kind of uncontrollable, temporary insanity, Lewis jumped on to the field as Moegle was flying by, and leveled him to the ground. Then the film shows Lewis retreating to the sidelines, ducking out of the way and trying to hide behind a teammate (like no one would see him?).

He didn't keep Moegle from scoring. The referees gave Rice the touchdown anyway. After the game, Lewis was forced to go to the Rice locker room and address their team and apologize for his unwise action. Lost in the jaw-dropping turn of events is that Lewis was one of Alabama's best players, and had actually scored a touchdown for the Tide earlier in the game.

The bizarre event drew national attention. The top entertainment variety show of the day, The Ed Sullivan Show, invited both players to New York to discuss what happened. In front of a national TV audience, Ed Sullivan asked Tommy the logical question: why did you do it? Lewis replied, "Mr. Sullivan, I was just *too full of Alabama, I couldn't help it.*"

Tommy's remarks reflect the mindset of the state into which I was born. Alabamians are full, sometimes to a fault, of team loyalty. Not surprisingly, other sensibilities can be dismissed.

When it comes to team loyalty, there is no in-between. You'd never hear a true Alabamian say, "Oh, I don't care who wins...Auburn or Alabama. Either one is fine with me." No, it doesn't work that way. I learned early in life that in regards to football loyalty there is no middle ground. Sort of like what we learned in Sunday School about money and God: you will either love one and hate the other, or the other way around. And if someone couldn't say that this football passion doesn't at least approach some kind of religious affection, then perhaps a better metaphor would be war.

Into this environment, I, Joe Billy Thompson was born in Sugar Hill, Alabama in 1962. As long as I could remember, I wanted to be a running back for the Auburn Tigers. I never said, "I'll play for Alabama if they offer me a scholarship." For me, the choice was clear. I would take up college residence at Auburn, the place that the poet Goldsmith called the Loveliest Village on the Plains. In that poem, Goldsmith said that Auburn was a place where "crouching tigers await their helpless prey." Somehow, some way, I would be an Auburn Tiger, overcoming helpless prey on the football field. And my life would proudly reflect the War Eagle tradition.

Something I learned early on was the meaning of one of Auburn's most important traditions and its place in school lore. Namely, I discovered why the team with a mascot of Tiger also shouts War Eagle. I was taught that though no one was quite sure, the most popular story had to do with a pet eagle in attendance with a Civil War veteran at the 1892 Auburn-Georgia game. (Which by the way, is an annual game still played and called the oldest football rivalry in the South. But I digress.) The eagle broke loose from its owner, and circled the field while Auburn continued driving towards the Georgia goal line, inspiring the team on to victory. Thus, the Auburn faithful have punctuated the air with a mighty crescendo of the cheer 'War Eagle!' for well over a century, a rallying cry built around a unified memory of America's greatest bird flying high, assisting the team to success.

My parents made sure that I would carry on the Auburn tradition of football excellence, stamping their desire upon me, starting with my name. I was officially born Joe Billy Thompson, not something more distinguished like Joseph William Thompson, the kind of name that the school principal reads out in full at a high school graduation and everyone says, "Whoa! Listen to that! I didn't know that was your full name. Fancy!"

Now, it has been customary in Alabama and throughout the South for some parents to expect their children to go by their first and middle names, and they are referred to in such a way that the two names sort of go together like Kathryn Ann, or Mary Grace, or John Ed, pronounced hurriedly so that the hearer can hardly tell if it's one or two names.

But the main reason I was named Joe Billy went much deeper than simple Southern tradition. Everyone in Alabama knew that Joe Willie Namath was arguably the greatest, or at least the most famous, quarterback in Crimson Tide history. Coach Paul Bear Bryant called him, "the greatest athlete I ever coached." My parents were determined that their son was going to make everyone forget Joe Willie. *Joe Billy* would be the ultimate Auburn football hero. As soon as some Crimson Tider would start bragging, an Auburn fan would no doubt say, proudly, "Yeah, but let me tell you about *Joe Billy*..."

Contrasted with the multitudes of insiders to the football culture of our state, you could always spot someone who "weren't from around here." They pronounced Auburn as if there was an emphasis on the "burn" and they even enunciated the noticeable "-rn" ending, rather than sort of a 'soft ending' of the "-rn", which was commonly heard. With the soft ending, the listener hardly noticed it. Thus, it was pronounced 'Auburn'. However, it was not unusual to find locals in Sugar Hill who varied the ending, and more often than not pronounced it Awbun, as in A-W-B-U-N. The city slickers who fly in and broadcast the occasional national football telecast of an Auburn game on channel 8 would pronounce it with the "burn", as in "Au-burn" and we always knew they "weren't from around here." It amazed me that they got paid big money for talking about Auburn football. And they didn't even know how to properly pronounce the team name.

When I was around 10, I loved to regularly daydream about my future glory days at Jordan-Hare Stadium. By the way, I noticed when foreigners pronounced the name of the stadium, the beginning of the word was something that sounded like "Jordan", as in "Jordache jeans." A true Auburn fan knew it was really pronounced Jerdun, as in Shug Jerdun (Shug, short for sugar, as in Sugar Hill), the greatest coach in Auburn history. That pronunciation of "Jordan" was yet another distinguishing mark of someone who was a cultural outsider.

My daydreaming often happened during something exciting like 5th grade Social Studies class, where we were studying the impact of llamas upon the economic development of South America. Suddenly, I would take the pitch on a 28 Sweep and dart and dance my way down the home team sideline, right in front of the coaching staff who were hollering in unison and wind-milling their arms, "Go! Go! Go!" I would juke out the Georgia Dawg linebacker who was 1st team all-Southeastern Conference, making him look absolutely pitiful in my wake. Then, I would simply run over the Tennessee Vol cornerback who was one of the top 25 players in America, and a certain NFL 1st round draft pick. Turning up the heat, I would outrun the safety from LSU, who according to *The Sporting News* magazine, was Mr. All-Universe. I would cut across midfield and outrun the whole vaunted Ole Miss secondary while the Auburn play-by-play announcer would scream, "He's to the 30! The 20! The 10, 5, touchdown, Au-buuuuuuurrrrrrrnnnn!" (Seems like in such moments the announcer always got away with various flavors of the "-rn" ending. But it didn't matter because he was one of the family, and everyone had grown used to him. That was just how it was shouted out on the radio. Everyone knew it wasn't normal speech.)

While 82,000 delirious War Eagle fans were on their feet and out of their minds, shaking a majestic array of blue and orange pompoms, I would wait for the referee to catch up with me in the end zone. Upon arrival (after a lengthy wait, I might add), I would sort of non-chalantly toss the ball to the out-of-breath referee who was signaling touchdown, or sometimes in my dreams just hand it to him as if to say, "You looking for this?" I wouldn't spike it like the attention-grabbing professional players, or gesture in the stands to some unknown fan, showing how great I was, or slam dunk it over the goalpost. I would just hand it to the ref as if the TD was the logically-expected outcome of what I had set out to do, and it was really no big deal. *Goodness, I had to come to grips with the fact that actually there was great pride in my humility.* It was just another reminder that it was hard to be humble when you're an Auburn Tiger.

Unfortunately, the curtain would invariably crash down on my stellar athletic performance, and my teacher would quickly turn me back to reality with an icy stare and an unmanageable request to summarize the impact of the llamas on highland Peruvian culture. As yet another sign of my veins flowing blue and orange and covered with pigskin, my knee jerk reaction emerging from this glorious and unmatched TD jaunt brought snickers, particularly from girls who were no doubt secret admirers of my exceptional football abilities, when I returned to the here and now and mumbled to my teacher, "Yes, ma'am! Llamas? Who are the

Llamas? Uh....Florida is the Gators, Kentucky, the Wildcats, Mississippi State, the Bulldogs...I'm not actually sure what conference the llamas are in, but I'll look it up in the library!"

She would then write a note and send me to the principal's office for punishment.

Poor lady. She would have to come to grips with one of the great questions of life: How do you tame an Auburn Tiger? I reckoned it wouldn't be easy for her.

3

The First Things First

One thing I heard more than once growing up was "There's a first time for everything!" As I started to compose this memoir, I realized how true that was. Life seems to be built on a series of firsts, either first experiences that are one and done, and don't go anywhere else, or firsts that open the door to lifetime involvement in an activity. As I've listened to my friends, some of them seem to regret a truckload of first things they got involved in. But not me. I have happy memories. My parents seemed to help me make wise choices, and good decisions. Whether one and done with the experience or something I have enjoyed throughout life, I am glad to look back and reflect on some major memories, that for the most part, bring a smile.

I remember, for example, the first time I saw Atlanta Stadium, home of the Braves. Our family drove to Atlanta to see the city and experience the "capital of the South" for a day or two of vacation. Unimaginable size! It was so different from Sugar Hill, I could hardly even make a reasonable comparison. As we drove into the city, on a madhouse road called an Interstate Highway, momma pointed and said, "There's where the Braves play!" Goodness. The stadium looked like an entire city by itself. We saw a Braves game that night; they took down Pete Rose and the Cincinnati Reds, and I loved every minute. Hank Aaron hit a home run. Eddie Matthews made a backhand grab of a tough lined shot and threw out a runner. Phil Neikro's patented knuckle ball was working. In between cheers, I ate so much concession stand food I must have looked like a bloated frog. But that didn't dampen my spirit. I was at The Big Show, and it became a lifetime memory.

I was 7 when man first walked on the moon. I remember it very clearly. It was on a Sunday night, and late. Daddy "made me" stay up and watch it happen on TV. Refused to let me go to bed, insisting that I plop down in front of grainy black and white transmissions from outer space. (How did they broadcast that, by the way?! Trying to wrap my head around that science still blows my mind.) I was leaving for church camp the next day, with at least an hour and a half drive ahead of me, and I wanted sleep. I don't remember anything else about that day of July 20, 1969; I assume we went to Sugar Hill Methodist Church that morning, and probably had returned at night as well, and that I had spent a humidity-filled Alabama summer afternoon playing baseball with my friends. (It was too early in the year for football, but it was always on my mind.)

Then it happened! Neil Armstrong stepped off the Eagle landing module and on to the moon's surface. Some probably guessed that at least a short, memorable speech was forthcoming, but I was too young and too inexperienced with big events in life to predict it. And I confess I don't remember Armstrong's famous words quietly entering our living room, "That's one small step for man; one giant leap for mankind." I hear the replay of those radio transmission exchanges now, and the words which get to me the most are actually the ones from the Capsule Commander back in Houston when the Eagle touched down on the moon,

"Tranquility [base], we copy you on the ground. You got a bunch of guys about to turn blue here. We're breathing again. Thanks a lot!"

I'm glad daddy insisted that I stay up and watch TV! Kind of funny to write those words; don't parents usually want their children to do the opposite: turn off the TV and go to bed?! He was a history lover, and he knew this 'first' was so epic, I would never forget my personal experience of witnessing men crawling out of a space craft after a 240,000-mile journey and taking steps on the moon's surface. (Rocks from that expedition were gathered and taken to schools for children to see them. I remember that clearly as well as they made the rounds in a display at Sugar Hill Elementary; the moon rocks looked like, well, rocks, but who had ever seen one of those before?)

As a post-script on the reflection of this once-in-a-lifetime event, I'm glad in an odd sort of way that one of my personal, quickly-recalled markers from the decade I was born, the turbulent 1960s, was not just about bad news. We had plenty of it. It seemed to keep coming. I was too young to remember where I was when our family heard that President Kennedy had been shot in Dallas. But I do know that people are still talking about it. I remember when Martin Luther King, Jr. was shot in Memphis. The killing of arguably the most famous black citizen in America was big news. He was in the news most days, it seemed, as he led peaceful protests against institutional, governmental, and cultural racism. But now, he had been silenced by a gunman at a motel in the Deep South. I remember when JFK's brother, Attorney General Bobby Kennedy, was shot, and also the governor of Alabama, George Wallace, who was campaigning in Maryland for the Presidential nomination. On the more positive side, I also remember the first Super Bowl; when Bill Russell regularly tangled with Wilt the Stilt Chamberlain under the basket; and, when World Series baseball games were only played in the daytime.

When I think of the 1960s, and consider life outside of Sugar Hill and my immediate interests such as football and school, I'm glad that what comes to mind is the moon landing, fulfilling JFK's pledge to put a man on the moon "by the end of the decade." Unparalleled achievement.

As we grow older, our vocabulary noticeably increases. That comes, of course, through conversations, and reading, and school work. I wish I could report that I learned a whole load of new words from studying and preparing for the Scripps-Howard National Spelling Bee. In elementary school, they gave us a printed list of possible words that we would be examined on. But they were so "big" and "long", I quickly lost heart and interest. No one I knew used those words, nor did they seem interesting. I didn't even advance out of my grade school. My 5th grade teacher thought that I had a chance, as I was a pretty good speller. I can still remember the look on her face, as she served as one of the judges, when I spelled 'eighth' as e-i-g-t-h. Made sense to me as a great spelling, but that was a laugh. They dismissed me from the stage, and that ended my spelling bee career. She never mentioned my downfall, and there was no participation trophy. I would just keep spelling the best I could. And, as a bonus outcome to my spelling bee study and subsequent failure, I'll add that I have never again misspelled the word 'eighth'.

Not uncommon to any of us is an introduction at some stage in our life journey to 'bad words.' I grew up in a house where my parents didn't use 'foul language' or 'cuss words', as they were known. I assume 'cuss' was some kind of mangling of the word 'curse', and I noticed that people freely substituted the phrase 'cuss words' and 'curse words', which best I could tell were the same thing.

Those vocabulary choices weren't too prevalent on TV in those days, so that wasn't much of a resource as the entry way into our minds. They were mostly absent from the visual entertainment we enjoyed. However, the Reagan Theater in town sometimes showed the epic movie, *Gone With the Wind*. My friends would emerge, giggling, and in hushed tones repeat the actor Clark Gable's final words, "Frankly my dear, I don't give a damn." (I didn't know till later that he was fined an exorbitant sum for uttering that word of damnation on the big screen.) It sounded so grown-up. My friends seemed to marvel at the verbal expression of this forbidden fruit, wondering if it would ever grace their lips, and they would be regarded as highly as Mr. Gable. I guess only time would tell.

I was taught that using those kinds of words was not acceptable. Mama was fond of saying that if someone talked that way, "It showed they were uneducated, with a limited vocabulary, and didn't have the ability to say anything differently." That was her perspective, and shared by my father, and I latched on to it. But that didn't stop me from *hearing* words that were spoken among my friends and not heard in my household, and wondering what they meant. Two instances come to mind.

One afternoon, when I was about seven, I was playing with one of my best pals, Jimmy Hightower. He was one year older, lived on my street, and we regularly romped together. We shared most things, even our specialty recipe of peanut butter sandwiches that were embedded with potato chips. We built forts in the woods, climbed trees, and traded baseball cards.

We were in his back yard playing with his pet snapping turtle he had found in a nearby creek, and had nicknamed Goliath. We had ceremoniously dragged it to his house, and let it wander around the chain-link fenced backyard. His father was out there with us, keeping an eye on us, and on the turtle, when Jimmy launched a curious broadside that Mr. Hightower was not expecting.

"Daddy, what's a *bitch*?"

Mr. Hightower was completely caught off guard. He exhibited a flinch with the raising of his eyes, and he inhaled slowly on his filter-less Camel cigarette. I knew the brand and the lack of filter. Jimmy had found some left unattended about two months before, and we had sneaked in the backyard for some puffs, just to see what the excitement was about. After vomiting solid for about half a minute, I wasn't sure.

Mr. Hightower exhaled even slower, filling the area of the backyard with smoke, no doubt contemplating how to help orient his eight-year old boy to a word obviously not uttered under their roof.

"Where'd you hear that word, Jimmy?"

"Jeffrey Morrison told me."

Another long drag on the cigarette. Another slow exhale, while Thoughtful Parent mentally formulated a responsible answer for his Grand Inquisitor.

When the smoke had billowed out of sight, Mr. Hightower had his answer and snapped, "I don't reckon you out to be playing with Jeffrey Morrison any more."

"Oh!"

Jimmy took that as a directive, but he didn't get the answer to his question. So, in repetitive childlike fashion, he posed it again.

"But what is a bitch, daddy?"

"It's a *female dog*, Jimmy!" he thundered.

Thus, Jimmy and I were clearly instructed: a female dog is a very bad thing, and should never be mentioned again. I wasn't sure what you call a male dog, but I knew then about female dogs, and I would avoid the canine-motivated subject.

The second cuss word recorded for posterity in my memoir had to do with the four-letter word, starting with 's', which I know now, roughly means 'manure.'

Our 4th grade class was playing softball during recess, and Big Tommy Tubingen (and I do mean big; he had repeated both the second and third grades) fouled off three straight pitches into the nearby woods. On the third one, he let loose with the 's' expletive.

I was standing in the on-deck circle. It was the first time I had ever heard that utterance. I said aloud to no one in particular, "*What does that mean?!*" James Freeman, the pitcher, immediately stopped the game, screwed up his face and forcibly blurted out, "It means you're gonna go to hell!"

I had the same immediate answer as Jimmy Hightower had upon hearing his father's reply to his query: "Oh!"

I was not far enough along in my biblical background or theological journey to even hint at an explanation of 'hell'. But from the way James had said it, I knew that it was a place to avoid, at all costs. That was one of my first ventures into theological learning. I got the message: Don't use the 's' word. Whatever it is, it indicated a place that you did not even want to think about, much less go to.

Someone asked me if I remembered my first kiss. Definitely! (As I was sharing memories of my life with an older friend, trying to get his input on what to include in my memoir, I asked him if he remembered his first kiss. He said he was so old, he didn't remember his last one! Whether kidding or not, I hope that doesn't happen to me.)

Touching lips with Sarah Walker was a physical experience like none I had ever known. Admittedly, I somewhat awkwardly leaned towards her, and she did the same towards me. But when we touched, I tingled, and lingered. She didn't resist, so I just stood there absorbing the joy. Now I know why so many people kiss! Great idea: this kissing, one of the innocent discoveries of youth.

It was after the football banquet of my junior year (and no doubt some readers will say that I waited a long time! Let's say I waited till the right time.) I had a big night at the banquet; in addition to receiving my varsity letter, I took home an award for Teammate of the Year. I guess my fellow players thought I was inspirational and encouraging. I certainly wouldn't win any of the MVP awards with guys like Jobab Robinson and Paul Washington on our team. More about them a bit later. But I was glad that I had made some kind of contribution, and was recognized for it. I assume that I share a conviction with most people, that it is ego-boosting to be recognized, and often leads to fond memories.

After the banquet, I was walking Sarah to the door, and we turned and embraced before saying good-night. I look back on that moment and can't say with confidence that it was planned. More like 'hoped-for', but it was hard to predict whether or not it would happen. It did. In one magical moment, she made me so glad I was a young man, alone with her. We remained friends, went out occasionally to Charlie's Pizza or to the Reagan Movie Theater, but never seriously dated. In addition to her beauty, she was very nice and fun to be around.

I realized that I liked girls who equally shared in the conversation. I was glad that I didn't have to force things and carry the load. Being with a member of the opposite sex in some kind of budding relationship or "dating environment" was awkward enough. Taking pressure off the conversation-side was helpful. Sarah was an engaging conversationalist, and very pleasant. Though we never moved to formalize our relationship and become exclusive with each other, we enjoyed being together. We were good friends, and neither of us expressed any regrets about the time we spent together.

My first serious girlfriend was Mary Harmon Makowski. A pretty brunette with the softest brown eyes I had ever seen. She seemed to always have a smile on her face. I had expressed my intentions of wanting to spend time together, and she reciprocated with an unequivocal yes. Once when we were alone, she whispered to me that I was "dreamy." Never thought of myself that way—but I reveled in it. She had played her cards face up. I had something which caught her eye, and she was not shy in telling me. That didn't scare me away! I latched on. It's easy to be around someone who thinks you're great, especially if you like them as well.

When I fell in love with her my senior year in high school, I didn't recognize that her name was significant: her parents had named her after Bear Bryant's wife. Obviously, they were Tide fans, and were determined that their daughter would be imprinted with an indelible mark. Can't blame the members of the Crimson Tide nation for claiming their territory.

Mary Harmon, as she liked to be called by the double name, brought up the subject of our possible long-term relationship, post-high school. Of course, she was headed to Tuscaloosa, the Capstone, for college, and I was off to east Alabama. Were we getting serious? Did we want to be serious? Surely we would meet other people at school; how would a long-distance relationship work out? We had lots of questions. Not many answers. We had never faced this kind of life-changing decision before. Funny how a college choice sets in motion a whole bunch of things you never thought about, another set of 'firsts' to negotiate. One of the big unanswered questions had to do with loyalties; with her being Alabama and me Auburn, could we survive a 'house divided'?

We soon discovered that we couldn't. Though we had expressed optimism that our deep love for each other (as carefully as two teenagers could define "deep love") would surely survive a few hundred miles of separation, she departed. Early in her first semester, she fell in love with a member of the Crimson Tide football team. Not a player, mind you, but one of the managers, or a "trainer", who worked the sidelines and helped all the players who were in the thick of the gridiron action. She had met him in her World History class, and something had clicked "like nothing I've ever known, Joe Billy", she feebly explained on the long-distance pay phone call from the Tutweiler dormitory lobby. And just like that, First Serious Girlfriend was gone. I wished her well and hung up. But it was hard to take. She went off with Trainer Boy, and I guess it was love everlasting. It was fun while it lasted, bitter for me when it ended. But time to move on. There would be other girls to meet.

The continuing game of making yourself vulnerable and expressing feelings and emotions for a member of the opposite sex suddenly felt like an unsolvable puzzle. I would have to consider things carefully before getting involved in another steady relationship. And thinking about what had happened with Mary Harmon, I should probably try to find an Auburn girl next time. There were plenty of those.

My first college football game was bigger than life itself. Daddy had decided when I was eight it was time to take me to Cliff Hare Stadium (before it was renamed Jordan-Hare) and introduce me to the crazy, chaotic world of Saturday afternoon major college football in the great state of Alabama. I was so excited the night before we made the journey to Auburn, my body refused to shift into sleep mode. The morning sun was a welcomed sight, as I knew the greatest day of my life had dawned. *I was going to an Auburn football game!* No dependence that day on television (should the game even be televised; most weren't), or radio, or a newspaper recap. I would watch it unfold in real time. Looking back on my youth, I would say it was probably the most special gift I ever received.

When we arrived, the Auburn band was performing in the streets outside the stadium, going through traditional pre-game routines, trying to get the crowd pumped for another mighty victory. Their music made me want to dance and shout and just start running! I had never seen or heard a band with that kind of talent, volume, and precision. I was enthralled. The pretty and athletic, gymnast-like cheerleaders also played their part in getting us all ready to go in and scream for the Tigers, as they accompanied the band down the street. The atmosphere was electric, so far superior to just watching the teams play on TV.

Our tickets weren't for seats down low near the field, but that was okay. We hiked up, and I mean way up, and as I look back now, we were so far up we could have almost used a Nepalese Sherpa guide to get there. But I didn't care. I took in all the sights and sounds from the upper half of the stadium. This was the most majestic view I had ever experienced, as my eyes scanned the stadium around and below me, and then above the stands and out of the stadium across the sprawling campus. I had gone to the game not knowing what to expect, but I did know that it would be marvelous. No disappointment there.

I was inside, where it was happening! I took it all in: the pregame punting and passing warmup drills, the extensive stretching by the offensive linemen, the important looking huddles and conversations that must have related to formations and strategies that would soon unfold. This was the big time. And I never wanted the day to end.

It finally did, mercifully coming to a conclusion for the hapless Mississippi State Bulldogs who couldn't keep up with the Auburn firepower. The Tigers were too much. In fact, the trouncing was so lopsided, folks started to leave at the beginning of the 4th quarter. *Really, y'all?! There is still football to be played!* I didn't know they were going to get a head-start on beating the traffic, or get to their post-game parties. Folks heading for the exits looked non-plussed. They didn't seem that excited to be in the big house. They had apparently seen what they had wanted to, especially with the drubbing in hand of the boys from the next state over. I had nowhere else to be. Daddy and I stayed till the final whistle. Even then, he had to pry me out of my seat.

I don't remember the drive home. The previous sleepless night had caught up with me, and all adrenaline had drained out. It was the best "tired" I had ever felt. Daddy told me that I had even slept through the drive-through at Hardee's. That was also a first.

Momma kept various scrapbooks of my life's achievements. Printed programs from school events. My horrible looking fourth-grade school picture, where my fake, forced smile and closed eyes should have called for a retake. The announcement in the local paper of the A and B honor roll. A picture of me getting my 2nd Class Award in the Boy Scouts at a court of honor. (I never did go higher than that rank. My best friends all started doing other things, and I lost interest.)

In a visit with my parents after I had already finished college, I came across a copy of a letter that I had written to *The Montgomery Advertiser*. Momma had kept this family treasure in addition to the newspaper invitation which caused me to write to them. The announcement read:

Be a Sideline Tiger for a day! The dream of a lifetime! One junior high student from the state of Alabama will be chosen on October 15 to watch the Auburn-Alabama game from the sidelines at Legion Field. The applicant must write a 150-word essay on why he or she would be the best sideline representative for the Tigers. Sponsored by the AU Alumni of Opelika. Mail the essay to: War Eagle, P.O. Box 1716, Montgomery, AL. 36104.

On the same page of the scrapbook was my entry:

"Dear Sirs:
My name is Joe Billy Thompson from Sugar Hill, Alabama. I'm in the eighth grade at Sugar Hill Junior High and I play fullback on the football team. My friends and coaches tell me I'm real good. Anyway, all my life I've dreamed of being an Auburn Tiger, and one day I know I'm going to play for them. In fact, my parents named me Joe Billy so that when I help Auburn win, Bama fans will quit talking about Joe Willie Namath. I can tell you from the bottom of my heart I know there's no one who wants to do this more than me. And, whether you choose me or not, I'm

still going to be pulling for Auburn when they beat the Tide. War Eagle!

Sincerely yours,
Joe Billy Thompson

I remembered that I had tried to imagine what it would be like if I won. Daddy and I had sat in the upper deck at the stadium at the one game we had attended; these people were talking about being on the sidelines! Right there with the monster-sized players in all their pads and Auburn blue jerseys. I had imagined that I would hear the coaches yell instructions, yell at their players for missed tackles, and yell at the referees. None of that could be heard from the stands. Why I might even get hit with some dirt when Auburn's tailback churned up the sidelines heading for the touchdown. When he came back to the bench amongst all the congratulations, I would reach up and smack him on the shoulder pad and say, "Great run." Sweaty Tailback would look down and smile and say to me, "Thanks, man." Then he would start bumping chests and patting helmets with his teammates. There I was, day-dreaming again about future glory at Auburn. Even as a junior high spectator.

However, my essay wasn't chosen. I read it now, and realize it wasn't that great, but I gave it my best shot. And who knew exactly what the judges were looking for? All I could do was try, and share my heart. Daddy often said, "Nothing ventured, nothing gained." Looking back, that was a motto that would come into play often in my days ahead.

Speaking of the days ahead, who would have guessed that after my brief flirtation in my youth with a short-lived announcement and invitation in *The Montgomery Advertiser*, that one day I would turn my love for writing into a career as a sports writer—at that very newspaper?! Looking back on it, it seemed like a natural fit. But when you're young, I reckon you have no idea how the puzzle pieces of life will fit together. One of the values of a memoir is seeing your life from a perspective of looking backwards, rather than forwards. Looking back often seems to be the way we learn things.

I also realized that no matter how much work it is to make the puzzle pieces fit, you can't run away from your passion. To develop that passion, you have to start somewhere, and then cultivate it. It's fair to say that responding to that random advertisement as a 13-year old was my first step towards a public proclamation of my love for expressing my views about college football.

In this catalog of 'firsts', I have tried to highlight just a few that have come to mind. For the record, I will state that there is one 'first' that is missing in my youth: the first day I cheered for Alabama. It's missing, because I never did that.

Couldn't imagine that I ever would.

4

The Beauty

Continuing with the topic of 'firsts', I note that right on the front end of growing adolescence, I made an important discovery: girls. One member of that extraordinary race of people that I did not know existed was one Betty Jean Asher. She captivated me long before I kissed Sarah Walker or dated Mary Harmon Makowski.

I was smitten. I had never felt like that before. It was such a deep crush, I could hardly function. I was so glad that when I met her, I had not yet had a severe bout with acne, the scourge of teenage-hood. I looked at myself in the mirror one day in my 10th grade year and thought I fit the bill of the Clearasil Poster Child. Luckily, it was in-between Betty Jean and Mary Harmon. Good riddance, teenage plague. It was hard enough to compete for someone like Betty Jean with everything going for you. Any setbacks popping up for mostly unknown reasons would make you work that much harder, or else just lead you to give up in frustration of trying to look good and be cool.

Betty Jean was an amazing creature. This blond hair, blue-eyed beauty slayed me. The odd thing, though, was how could a girl this beautiful not be from Alabama? Her family, I had heard, had moved down from Ohio or Iowa or some other far-away place and she was just settling in during that eighth-grade year. In a small town like Sugar Hill, foreigners attracted a lot of attention. On top of that, there was no way that a girl this gorgeous could go unnoticed.

Reflecting on my daddy's words, "nothing ventured, nothing gained", I thought long and hard about how to get her attention. I wondered if she liked football? Maybe she would come to one of our junior high games. We did have one class together, but I sat clear on the other side of the room. There was no way she would notice me from there. I was too shy to call her on the telephone. And that idea had its own built-in trickery, as my family would be listening in around the edges with our centrally-located telephone in the living room. (Not that long ago, our family had abandoned the "party line", a telephone line shared by multiple houses around us, as it was a household cost-saving measure. Even so, the one phone in our house was a danger zone for any possible romantic advances.) Besides I would have to somehow get her number first, and that would take some work. I would have to own up to the fact that I was interested enough to want to call her. Any of my friends who found out that I had called her would give me interminable grief. Then I would have to sidestep the fact and lie and say "I don't like her, I just wanted to talk to her," or some such lame excuse. I decided the phone route wouldn't work. But I did find out where she lived, and so I started walking by her house going home from football practice.

Usually when I walked by, there was no one stirring outside. No one working in the yard, though it looked well kept, and no one out on the porch. But one afternoon as I was walking by slowly I noticed her coming out of the house.

There she was! My heart started racing as I tried to unloose my tongue and figure out something intelligent to say. Before I knew it, I called out to her with a shaky voice, "Hello, Betty Jean." My heart was in my throat and my voice quality sounded more like I was in pre-puberty than a strapping eighth grader, but at least I got the words out.

She quickly smiled and came off the veranda, down the sidewalk, and near the house. Those beautiful white teeth! I had never seen them up close. They were yet another confirmation that every part of her was perfect.

"Good afternoon." Her words flowed effortlessly, smoothly. They hit the mark. She had spoken! To me!

I stopped breathing. Still barely able to talk, I mustered, "I'm Joe Billy Thompson. We're in math class together, but I sit at the other end of the room."

"Oh, yeah. Hi. I don't think we've formally met. I'm Betty Jean Asher."

She had said more than just "hi" and I was enjoying every second of this. She sounded mature, confident, grown up. My momma's words had been pressed down into my mental faculties, that girls were more mature than boys at the same age. I realized in Betty's Jean's presence the truth of that statement. I was no match for her. But I wasn't going to do something dumb like say, "Well, nice talking to you. See you later. I gotta go. (And besides, you're much more mature than me!") I didn't have to go. I could have stayed there forever.

"We just moved here from Pennsylvania and my family lives right there in that two-story."

Ah, so it wasn't Ohio or Iowa, but Pennsylvania. None of my friends knew the true story but me. I was now way up on them.

"We live the other side of town," I feebly said. I was still trying to find my proper breathing rhythm. My house didn't compare to hers, but that didn't actually matter at the moment.

I couldn't believe she was talking to me. The slight breeze was moving her delicate hair and I was convinced that I never wanted that conversation to end. I had admired her from a distance, and though my friends would laugh their heads off if they knew, and heap scorn by the bushel load, I had secretly contemplated what it would be like to be married to her, even though she had not spoken to me until this very moment. She definitely fit the bill of the kind of wife I was hoping for. This surprise encounter and unprecedented opportunity to gaze close up at her was just about all the proof I needed.

Hoping to impress her with my budding athletic prowess, and sensing my confidence building by the moment, I said, "Do you like football? I play running back for the junior high team and we've won all our games so far."

"Oh, I love football." With a chuckle she continued, "Daddy made sure of that."

"I don't know her daddy," I quickly surmised to myself, "but if he loves football, I like him—even if he is from up north."

She continued. "Yeah, we moved to the right state. We may have lived in Pennsylvania, but I was born here. Daddy has always been a Bama man. He coached for Bear

Bryant when Alabama won the national championship in 1964. The star player on that team was Joe Willie Namath. You might have heard of him? He was a great quarterback, and he was from Beaver Falls, Pennsylvania. After graduation, Joe Willie invited him up there, and told him it would be a great place to live and raise a family. Daddy checked it out and agreed. Anyway, after college daddy went into business for himself selling insurance. We moved back down here because daddy said it was just time to come home. We loved Pennsylvania, but Alabama is a better place for us."

I was motionless, digesting the words with pain. When she said she was a Tide fan, I couldn't have gone into more shock than if I had just watched my favorite hunting dog get run over by a pickup truck. *How could a girl this beautiful be loyal to the enemy?*

She said a few more things, but my mind was far away. I had heard someone say that in a wedding the preacher says something about have and hold, love and cherish till death do us part. That wasn't going to be possible. How could I do all that having, and holding, and cherishing with a lady with whom I knew that I couldn't carry on a conversation on a particular Saturday in November for the rest of my life?

As I struggled to gather my thoughts, one thing was suddenly obvious: unless Betty Jean Asher had a major life change, as far as I was concerned, the wedding was off.

5

The Moon Pie

For the reader to properly understand the context of my growing-up years, it's important that I share some stories that demonstrate the unusual and extraordinary passion that Alabamians have for college football. Many such stories about certain people come to mind. My Uncle Joe is a case in point.

Uncle Joe's given name was Robert Joseph Thompson, and he was affectionately known as "Moon Pie" Thompson. He was a large man, blessed with an enormous intimidation factor. He had gotten the name Moon Pie from his prowess at ingesting the notable Southern sweet treat. As his neighbors said in typical Southern syntax, "Joe loves him some moon pies." I have no idea how he did it, but legend has it that when he was in high school, he once ate 14 moon pies in two minutes flat at the Dale County Fair. He also washed down those gummy, cardboard-like, chocolate-coated delicacies with a suitable flow of RC Cola, or as some of the locals pronounced it, R-O-C Cola. I never was sure why. (Maybe it was because the "R" stood for Royal and the next letter in Royal was "O", while the "C" was for Crown, Royal Crown Cola. I don't know. Only guessing. I did know it was the drink of choice with moon pies, however it was pronounced.)

Word got 'round about his note-worthy feat, and he got invited by the organizing committee to the Mobile Moon Pie Drop on New Year's Eve. Let the northerners in New

York City have their Ball Drop in Times Square, where thousands of pick-pockets roam freely. We southerners have something much more fun: the Moon Pie Drop. Southern food, southern charm, southern drama, southern welcoming. New Year, glad to meet you! Let's start it off right with the bread of fellowship, the moon pie! And, wait: can anyone think of a better poster boy representative than Uncle Moon Pie himself? Sounds like a public relations job made in heaven.

Story goes that Uncle Moon Pie was the hit of the party. Anyone with that kind of size, that kind of reputation, that kind of love for all things Southern, he had to be a good guy. Why not make him the Grand Marshall of the New Year's Eve party? Don't stop the rumor mill. Sure, in his youth he had only eaten 14 in 2 minutes. But what did it hurt when *The Mobile Press Register* said it was not 14, but 21 moon pies in a minute and a half? I mean, really, did that cause any harm? No one could come close to his record anyway. Why not just put it out of reach through public journalism? The legend lives. And grows. Uncle Moon Pie showed that it was great to be a southerner. And an Alabamian on top of that.

Uncle Moon Pie was the quintessential Auburn fan. My dad's older brother wasn't just a die-hard Auburn fan, but he was the gold standard, the supreme example. This was demonstrated in various ways, all of which added up to Super Fan. He had tons of Auburn paraphernalia, Auburn gadgets, the proud display of tickets from about 200 different Auburn games he had attended. His third wife had tolerated his obsession more than the other two. They had fled when they realized they couldn't keep up with his War

Eagle Pride; no hard feelings, but they both reportedly said the same thing upon exiting: "This marriage ain't working."

Wife number three did draw the line with Orange and Blue curtains in their bedroom. She said it felt more like a boys' locker room than a place of quiet repose and marital love, and she just wouldn't have it. After losing two wives, he gave in and had the off-white ones restored to the curtain rods. It must have been a weak moment, but she traded the rights to the curtain colors for the naming of their twin sons. He promptly declared they were Bo and Beasley, named after two of his all-time favorite Auburn players, Bo Jackson and Terry Beasley. She tried to protest, but to no avail. "What's wrong with John and David?" she argued. But in the end, a deal is a deal. Auburn mania prevailed.

Besides his obsessive attendance record, and his hefty contributions to the Auburn Athletic Department, there was the constant splash he made by alternating Orange and Blue blazers that he wore to work every day. But to top off his fan status, Uncle Moon Pie demonstrated what I came to find out was the personal position that sealed his status as quintessential fan: *he loved Auburn, and he hated everything Alabama.* He rejoiced when Alabama lost at anything. Even women's gymnastics. His two favorite football teams, as the old saying goes, were Auburn, and whoever was playing Alabama that Saturday.

While he was cheering Auburn on in person from his season-ticket seat at Jordan-Hare, his transistor radio with an appropriate earpiece was communicating the outcome of the Tide's tangle with their latest foe. He could be at the Auburn game, and oddly at the same time he was cheering his lungs out for Ole Miss, Miss State, or Southern Miss, any

Mississippi school that had the misfortune of playing the mighty Crimson Tide on that Saturday. He cheered for those Mississippi boys like they were long lost relatives arriving on a trans-Atlantic ship, docking at Ellis Island for immigration into the USA.

Funny thing, though, it didn't add up: when those same Rebels, Bulldogs, or Golden Eagles played Auburn, he pulled against them like they were the very Devil in the flesh. How did that work? And what about the Kentucky Wildcats? They have beaten Alabama exactly once since 1922. Odds are not good that Bama-haters will have a pleasant and gloat-filled Saturday any time soon with the news coming out of Lexington, KY. Didn't stop Uncle Moon Pie. He cheered on the old Kentucky Blue like this could actually, really, no-fooling, be *the* year.

Good luck with that.

Since every team that played against Alabama usually lost, Uncle Moon Pie spent a lot of time in the autumns moping. That was despite the fact that he hollered and screamed and half-terrified the neighborhood when Bama's opponents didn't respond too well to his fanatical urgings via his television set. I think he knew the TV was not a two-way communication device. But I was never sure of that.

Take for example what happened one New Year's Day when Uncle Moon Pie was watching the Crimson Tide play Texas A&M in the Cotton Bowl. I had invited myself over, but was sitting on the other end of the couch. He could get a bit rowdy. Whenever the Aggies scored, or got a turnover, he would jump up from the couch, race to the front door, open it, and shout up in the sky as loud as he could, "Go you Aggies!!!" When Bama scored he sulked and fussed and made excuses, or blamed the referees. I noticed the veins on his neck were bright red. Or were they crimson-colored?

If Auburn happened to lose, it was more than just a double mope. It was something akin to morbid depression. That was something like I had read about in Civics class; it was what was called cruel and unusual punishment. I think that's what they called it.

Things got out of hand one Saturday so severely that a neighbor called the law on him. She—a Miss Bowman who lived 3 doors down—had heard Uncle Moon Pie hollering the memorable words, "Hit him harder!" And, "Don't let him up until you kick his behind so hard he'll never forget it!"

Within about five minutes of her phone call, a sheriff's deputy showed up in the driveway. Exiting the car forthwith, he ran to the front door and rapped on it.

No answer.

He rang the doorbell.

No answer.

Those actions were accompanied by the usual law enforcement pronouncement, "Sheriff! Open up!"

No response.

He kept banging away until the door cracked open. There was Uncle Moon Pie, one hand on the doorknob, another holding a pan of mac and cheese dripping over the edge, but his back was to the door and his eyes glued to the TV set. He mumbled, "Can I help you? Oh, c'mon! You missed that tackle, son! Don't make me come over there!"

When the deputy announced that he was with the sheriff's department and answering a complaint of domestic dispute, at first Uncle Moon Pie didn't seem to hear him. Then the deputy repeated himself. Uncle Moon Pie paused in his absorption of the ongoing football views from the Loveliest Village on the Plains and said, "What was that?"

"A domestic disturbance complaint. Who's here with you?"

"Who's here? Just me!"

"Are you sure? I got a call that there is a serious altercation taking place."

The roar of the crowd temporarily halted Moon Pie's engagement with the deputy sheriff. He yelled at the TV, "You all look horrible! Good night above."

Undeterred, the deputy waded back in. "Who is here with you?"

"Are you seriously asking me that? I live alone, and none of my friends want to watch the game with me. Say I'm too loud and unruly. I don't even know what you are talking about."

Checking his notepad, the deputy continued, "Says here that you were overheard—and I say overheard shouting, not just talking—to declare you were going to hit someone, and that somebody was going to get their rear end kicked..."

Moon Pie was in a state of disbelief. He realized who the busybody was, and starting to boil, he announced, "Are you trying to infringe on my rights of free speech? I can say anything in my house that I want to, at any time, whether anyone is here or not—which they aren't. You try to take away my rights, and I'll be glad to sue you, and see you in court. Is that what you want to do?"

The deputy was not expecting this full frontal assault. He was totally confounded by this point. He asked for a third time, "Are you sure there's no one here with you?"

"If you ask me that question one more time—especially since the answer is the same one that I gave you when you first asked—I'm calling a lawyer. You are really starting to irritate me."

Trying to do his duty and not appear intimidated or sheepish, the deputy tried to peer and peek around the massive frame of the Moon Pie, and perhaps catch a glimpse of some poor, abused soul who was hiding in the shadows, no doubt with blood oozing out of open wounds. He couldn't believe someone would call in a domestic disturbance complaint over someone shouting at his TV set during an Auburn game. Were they serious? Was this some kind of prank? But he had to face the fact that the case against Moon Pie was unraveling faster than an anchor rope going through his hands to the bottom of Lake Martin.

Exasperated, the deputy sheriff didn't know what to say. He simply turned away and went back to his car. He needed to call this in to the office and tell them what happened, but he wasn't sure how to say what he needed to.

When he opened the car door, he heard shouting coming from Moon Pie's living room. "An interception! Really! Just as we were driving! I thought we threw enough interceptions last week to last us a month! Pull him out of there, coach!"

The bottom line was that the deputy sheriff had been eaten up by an eccentric Auburn fan named Moon Pie. That would be tough to document.

6

The Unfortunate Superstar

I was envious of my junior high football teammate, Paul Washington. I looked the part of developing adolescent, but Paul didn't. If you saw him in a grocery store, you would think he was probably a junior, maybe a senior, in high school. He didn't strut or prance around, or show off or show out. He just had a quiet, solid demeanor. He was self-confident and mature. He separated himself from the rest of us in terms of ability and performance. As a football superstar, he didn't just play wide receiver, he dominated the game.

He had thighs like the proverbial tree trunks. His upper body strength was amazing, though I rarely saw him work out in our pitiful, makeshift sort of weight room. Many of us labored there, sweating our heads off, and doing pull ups and arm dips and sit ups and lifting free weights, such as they were. Trying to do something, anything, with those scrawny arms and non-existent core muscles. Paul just showed up at practice in his chiseled upper body. He already had his man body, and for most of the rest of us, well, we had junior high boy bodies.

And Paul had facial hair! It was very noticeable to us in junior high. We all wanted facial hair, but for some reason, it just wouldn't grow. (Occasionally we could find a naïve soul who bought the proverbial bill of goods, and convince him in the locker room after practice and showers that if he smeared toothpaste on his upper lip, his moustache hairs would grow out. Of course they didn't, and we howled behind his back. When found out and confronted by someone in authority, like a coach or parent, we did not confess our sins, but played dumb. "Who, me? Why would I tell someone that?" Asking the "Why would I?" question seemed not to be an outright lie, but in the spirit of the question and getting down to who was responsible, it was.) Back to Paul, he needed no such artificial—or fictional—stimulants. He had facial hair to die for. His face said he was a man. Already. In the eighth grade! He simply needed a razor. Good grief. What's next? Is he going to vote in the upcoming general election?

We had one other guy in our class like that, Georgie Miller. But Georgie was 17 years old in the eighth grade and now in his second year of driving to school every morning. He regularly had, in turn, and one at a time, a parade of young ladies beside him when he did. Having a driver's license in the 8th grade was definitely a difference maker. Georgie had some amazing sideburns and facial array, but he was not a normal junior high guy. That face regularly absorbed adoring kisses from the young ladies who were just learning how to express themselves in that way. Good for him.

Back to Paul. His feet were incredibly fast. After catching a pass, he didn't run around defenders; he ran over them. He punished them with his presence. I was watching him in practice one day. I'll sewanee, if he didn't get the pitchout and run down the left side line and bowl over not one, not two, but three defenders. They were laying on the ground holding their helmets, stomachs, legs, any body part that happened to be in the way when this freight train got up to full speed. In a word, Paul was ridiculous. His hands were so sure, it was as if they were made of flypaper, or a mouse sticky pad. A quarterback would throw him a pass and if Paul touched the ball, he caught it.

Coaches salivated in his presence. They built their passing game around him. He was one of those kids picked out of the herd very early who was legitimately going on to play major college football one day. And we would all remember Paul and say, "I knew him way back when."

One thing I haven't mentioned about Paul was that he was black.

I don't care how good you were at football in the state of Alabama in the early 1970s. If you were black, you were behind the eight ball. Which is also black, I might add.

You can probably tell from my memoir of admiration for Paul Washington that I envied him. But it's fair to say that while I would like to think I was color-blind, and saw Paul as Paul, a young man my age, a friend, a nice respectable member of the community, one who practiced "yes, sir" and "no, ma'am" in his conversations, and who came from a great family, the truth is that being black in Bama in the 1970s put you in a different category. Even if you were an amazing football player.

From the small southeast Alabama town of Ozark, the Crimson Tide found its first black scholarship football player named Wilbur Jackson. Coach Bryant had pledged in the early 1960s that he would keep the Alabama team segregated going forward. But he changed his mind when he saw the new dimension that black players brought to the game. Purposefully, it's said, Coach Bryant scheduled the Alabama-USC game in 1970 in Birmingham. He wanted the state to witness the arrival of the great Sam Bam Cunningham of USC, and the dominance that this black man brought to the backfield. Story is told that Coach Bryant had Sam visit the Tide locker room after the game—after destroying the Bama defense—and shake hands with his players. Bryant knew that black players were the future of Alabama football, and he was heard to utter and mutter the memorable words, "We got to get us a black football player." Did they ever. Jackson began his dominating performance in 1971, and over three seasons, he averaged more than 7 yards per carry *for his career.* Unreal. A Tide record that probably won't ever be broken.

But Bryant's earlier declaration of segregation was cast in the shadow of famous governor George Corley Wallace who had stood in the doorway in June of 1963 at the state University at Tuscaloosa, denying admission to the first black students, and had vowed, "Segregation now, segregation tomorrow, segregation forever." Many whites cheered him on. Many whites recoiled in horror. That's kind of how it was in a racially prejudiced society; your background influenced your support. You better know which side you're on. And you had better have a good reason for being on it. Talking to my friends, I never could quite tell why they were on the segregation side, other than that's how they were raised. That was their reason.

Heck, one of my friends proudly crowed in our neighborhood one day when we were all discussing the impending integration of public schools in Sugar Hill, "Daddy said if the blacks go to our school, he's gonna put me in the Christian school." 'Christian school' was code for private, whites-only education. Supposedly, the quality of education was better. But did anyone really know that for sure? Had it ever been proven? Or was it just accepted that if it were private, and not public, then it had to be better?

At least it would be safer. People like Paul Washington wouldn't be allowed in to the Christian school. Christian school kids would be exempt from public school integration. Didn't make sense to me, but that was the way things worked around here.

I remember one day telling Paul, "Let's go over to the country club in Scottsboro and go swimming. I hear they've got a swell pool. I can get us a ride over there, and I have a friend that's a member and will let us in." Paul looked me at like I had just had a mental breakdown. He had no comprehension as to what I was saying. Did I really think that I could get us into the whites-only country club? Like he wouldn't be noticed? We would just saunter up to the front gate and I would say, "Oh, hi, yeah, me and my friend Paul here want to come swimming today! My buddy, Jeffrey Reynolds, said it was fine to come...no problem...by the way, how tall is your diving board?" That sort of introduction would be met with a stern reply with no nonsense, no wiggle room, no negotiation, and the country club sergeant-at-arms pointing his finger at me: "You can swim; but he dang sure can't swim."

Why? Only one reason: Paul Washington was black. His recent history was that he had to drink out of a separate water fountain. He had to use a restroom marked Colored. His daddy had to sit in the back of the bus. And on this particular day, it was clear to Paul, and he convinced me it was true: he would have to find a different swimming hole. All because he was black.

It didn't matter if he was destined for the NFL.

Talk about an education. I didn't need to go to a Christian school. The education I was getting was enough for me.

7

The Blue-Chip Recruit

I thought Paul Washington was something. Jobab Robinson was an even bigger something. The small town of Sugar Hill, Alabama, for some odd reason, had two of the greatest high school football players on one team that you could ever imagine existed. It was like having two All-Pros on the same offense. And as good as Paul was, Jobab was a notch ahead, the best high school football player ever. Period.

True, his name was odd. His daddy originally wanted to name him Cameron. Said it sounded 'solid'. But then he decided it was too plain, too ordinary. He wanted to name him something that no one else was named. So, in his Bible reading one day in 1 Chronicles, he came across the name Jobab. And that's how his newly-born son went through a name change, from Cameron to Jobab. Just like that. As he grew up we called him J (and it was written with no punctuation), or JB, or JBB. Nobody close to him called him Jobab, but he was good with it. He was legendary, and was known simply by letters of his first name. That's pretty special.

He was not only the greatest football player any of us had ever seen, but he was the smartest guy in our school. Genius level. We didn't imagine anyone could be that smart. Nor, in the same body, be the greatest football player we knew, or imagined we would ever meet. He was the kind of guy you read about in a magazine, and you wondered if it were true all they said about him. And he was living right here amongst us mere mortals!

His senior year, he rushed for 45 touchdowns. That's more than 4 per game in a ten-game season. He averaged just under 300 yards rushing per game. That figure did not take into account that he saw action in only 3 fourth quarters all year. The reason was simple: with J and Paul Washington on the same offensive unit, providing balance to the running and passing games, we, the Sugar Hill Bulldogs, annihilated our opponents. No contest. A perfect 10-0 season. Best team in our classification—maybe any classification—in the state of Alabama.

He also ran track. One fact about him says it all: he had verified world class speed in the 60-yard dash. He covered that distance in just over 6 seconds. And he was only in high school, for Pete's sake! What college track coach wouldn't love to him at the mark? But how could a guy who was 6 feet 4 inches tall, weighing 225 pounds, move down the track that fast? Well, he did have a 32-inch waist, very long legs, and a motor that wouldn't stop running. He was chiseled, sort of like what I had seen in pictures of the sculptures of a Greek god. Girls almost fainted when he walked by them in the hall at school.

And then there was his brain. Never made a B in his life in any class, none recorded on any report card, from grades 1 through 12. None of us knew anyone like that. Was he taking the same tests we were? He had declared to his friends when we were in the 8th grade that he was going to be a doctor. That didn't surprise us. Others had said the same, but for them it seemed more like a dream or a wish rather than a concrete plan, and we just kind of smiled and went along with them. But with J it was different. When he talked about being a doctor, you knew he meant business.

On top of being a doctor, he decided in high school that he wanted to also be a research scientist who would one day find a cure for cancer. He wasn't going to just put out a shingle on Fifth and Main that said, "Dr. Moore, Family Practice", but he was going to be in the running for a Nobel Prize in Medicine. Couldn't fault him for his aspirations and ambitions! He was dreaming big, and not just talking the talk. When he took the ACT exam, and received a perfect score, recruiting directors were knocking down his door to get to him. Especially when they found out that he was black. Colleges were starting to implement quotas based on race, and J was at the top of the list.

Obviously, his football field exploits drew attention from coast to coast. Every in-state school wanted him. Bama consistently called and came by. I was hanging out with J at his house playing chess one afternoon when the phone rang and the Bama recruiter called with the message, "Just happened to be passing through Sugar Hill; mind if I stop by?" J said ok, but you could tell he was a little agitated. He was weary of the attention, and the postcards, the calls, the letters (which all said the same thing, "You are the greatest, and we can't live without you! Hope you come join us at wherever.") They were more than just polite inquiries. Each inquirer wanted to close the deal. J was their guy, and he told me they promised him everything. Introduction to girls, extra spending money that might be available, use of a car on the weekends. He would start at tailback as a freshman and would probably make all-SEC. He was destined for the NFL; come join us and we will get you there!

Why, one of our former coaches was on the staff of the Miami Dolphins and he's got connections, and he knows you are a can't-miss…and so it went. In those days, he was called a Blue Chip recruit. Now he would be a five-star recruit. And that's only because they don't have six-star recruits.

I'll speak for myself: I was thrilled when the doorbell rang and the Bama recruiter walked in. I didn't care that he was Alabama, and I was Auburn; I was in the presence of a real, big-time college football coach. It didn't get much better than that.

The recruiter introduced himself as Wesley Smith. Tall, blond, certain. Carried an air of importance and sophistication. He was a member of the staff of the legendary Bear Bryant. Goodness! He worked with Coach Bryant? He knew him? I was going to stick around for this. Despite my love for Auburn football and desire to be a college headliner myself, by the time we got to late high school years, it was pretty apparent that some of us had it, and most didn't. I was part of the most. J was part of the some. And being in the same room with him and Wesley Smith was probably as close as I would get to a behind-the-scenes look at how football greatness starts on the next level. Even if Bama was in focus, I was in awe.

"Jobab," he said confidently about 30 seconds after entering the living room, "can't wait to see you at Tuscaloosa this fall."

J had not yet declared his intentions. Or, if he had, he hadn't told any of us his plans. But J looked him right in the eye and said simply, "Not sure I'm coming."

"What do you mean you aren't sure?! You want to wear the crimson and white jersey don't you? Oh, I know, we talked about your teammate Paul Washington coming with you, and we are working with him, also nailing down a scholarship offer...he's tremendous..."

"No, it's not about Paul, though I do want to continue to play football with him. He's an amazing athlete, and an even better person. I have no doubt he would do great at Bama and be a tremendous asset to your program." His direct, to-the-point reply, left no doubt that he had a well-thought out reason for everything he was saying.

"Well, is there anything that's giving you hesitation, anything we can talk about or work through? I want to make sure that all of your questions are answered, and that any possible reason that would keep you from coming to Alabama will be dealt with swiftly and thoroughly."

J had a ready answer. "I have been thinking a lot about what life must be like for a student athlete at a top school in the SEC. Great opportunities and national exposure. Experience that promises to open doors in the days ahead. A pedigree from a top school that will carry weight for a lifetime. However, I see prejudice around me every day. I know what it's like to be a black man in a white-man majority world. I'm not sure that kind of stage is going to contribute to my life goals."

Recruiter Smith was taken aback by this. He wasn't expecting this kind of reasoning. In his previous dozen conversations or so, J had never raised this kind of hesitation. But as a recruiter who routinely heard complaints and queries, he had learned to take them in stride, smooth over the trouble spots and keep everyone moving forward together, hopefully leading up to a name signing on the dotted line of the national letter of commitment.

"Is there an incident in particular that you are referring to?"

"No," J said. "But I have been imagining what might happen. The first time I fumble, I'll get some mail that will read, 'If you can't hold on to the football better than that, boy, then take the next boat back to Africa.' Or, 'If you fumbled a watermelon as often you do a football, your feet would be a splattery mess.' I know there are rednecks out there, and they are probably for the most part ignorant fools, but I don't excuse them. And I wouldn't put it past them to burn a cross in my yard some night if I make a mistake and we lose a close game. Or, what about if I didn't make a mistake but was fingered as the scapegoat and what I should have done to avert defeat at the hands of some hated enemy."

He paused. His eyes left the shocked face of Recruiter Smith and he said, "I'm not sure I'm ready for those possibilities. I love to play football, and I'm pretty good at it..."

"Pretty good at it!" Recruiter Smith exploded. "You are the best high school running back I've ever seen. You've got 'can't miss' stamped all over you. Look at your mailbox! It's not filling up because you are just 'pretty good'."

"I appreciate that affirmation, and I've worked hard to get to this point of athletic success. But I want to be a student athlete, in the truest sense of that term. You need to know that I'm not planning on a career in the NFL. I want the best college education possible."

I looked at Recruiter Smith. A bead of sweat was building on his forehead. Was he hearing crazy talk, or was this kid serious?

"If I sign with Alabama, will I get the best education possible to pursue my life goal of being a medical doctor? I want to not only be an M.D., but I want to use that training and professional position to enter into the world of a molecular biology research scientist and find a cure for cancer."

Recruiter Smith was obviously stunned. It took him a momentary pause to counter, best he could, in stride, like he heard this every day from high school running backs destined for the Saturday afternoon big show on TV. "We take academics very seriously for our student athletes at Alabama. We will do all we can to help you succeed in your classes. We have study halls, tutors, late-night help. Coach Bryant makes sure of that."

"I'm sure you will help me," J replied. "But I don't just want to take and pass classes. I want to excel in my field of study. I'm simply wondering if the pressure of playing for a big-name school in the South will help me to achieve my life goals. That's all."

Recruiter Smith blanched. He had literally visited every county in the great state of Alabama. He had sat in hundreds of living rooms, and pretty much said and heard the same thing on every visit. But this was a first. Jobab Robinson was way off script. And he wasn't sure how to handle him. I know he was frantically thinking what would it be like when he went back to Coach Bryant and said that their number one recruit was more interested in curing cancer than in beating Tennessee every third Saturday in October for the next few years.

He fumbled for words to try to keep the conversation going. I thought he was going to ask for a paper sack to breathe into to keep from hyperventilating.

"So...what are you thinking at this point?" This was Smith's first find-a-cure-for-cancer recruit, and he didn't know where to go next.

"Since you asked, I'm honestly thinking about going to Sewanee, Tennessee to the University of the South."

Smith reactively sputtered out "huh?!", the kind of "huh" you might hear when someone looks at their bank statement and finds out their account was drained of all cash overnight, and their brain is trying to make sense of that jolt. Jobab didn't break his stride, but continued.

"By the way, you may know they are an original member of the SEC. Their 1899 team was voted the greatest college football team of all time, not only going undefeated and only once-scored-on, and that by Auburn, but they won 5 games in 6 days. G.O.A.T, greatest of all time, is pretty impressive, even if it was a long time ago."

J paused and smiled. "I've talked to their coach, and he would welcome me to their team. On top of that, they have an amazing pre-med program, and their lead Biology professor just won a national award for research in cell mutation in the liver. I've read three of his published articles, and I am eager to meet him. I'm actually hopeful he will be my faculty advisor."

Recruiter Smith blinked, exhaled, and then suddenly assumed a defensive posture. He looked like he had taken a linebacker's forearm shiver to the jaw, but was instinctively bouncing back, quickly. He wasn't letting Jobab go without a fight. His defensiveness showed.

"University of the South! Are you kidding! They are a Division 3 school. They don't even give athletic scholarships! You want to play Millsaps, Montevallo, and Po Dunk U on Saturdays, or do you want to play against LSU and Auburn every year?"

"I've told you, coach, I love football, and I am honored that Bama wants me. But I get the feeling that Bama wants me because I will help Bama meet their goals, as a team and as a school, rather than being wanted because they will help me to meet my goals. And I get it; a scholarship means you are paying my way, and I'm grateful for that. In a sense, I guess you would own me, though I won't read too much into that term. I'm only eighteen years old, and I know that life is not all about me. The University of Alabama is a great school, and I would get a good education, and I would never think or say otherwise. But the pressure to deliver the goods on the gridiron, as a black man in a still-white-man's-world, feels like a distraction, to be honest."

Recruiter Smith was obviously going through his brain to figure out which card to play next. He had pretty much played them all face up on the table. In his business, representing the Crimson Tide, he rarely lost a recruit. If Bama offered, the young man usually accepted. It was the dream school for so many. Every year, thousands wanted to join the football team; only a handful were chosen. The reasons for the chosen few going elsewhere had to be pretty well-founded, and they were rare. He couldn't think of ever losing one even to a Division 2 school. Maybe to Tennessee or Auburn or Notre Dame or Texas. Anyone who caught Bama's eye was certainly going to a top school somewhere in the country. But to lose someone to a Division 3 school?! That would be akin to downright blasphemy!

He could just see himself reporting back in from his recruiting trip.

"Well, Smith, did Jobab sign?"

"Uh, no, sir. He's going somewhere else."

"*Darn it.* Where?"

"Sewanee."

There would be silence.

Then his boss would say, "Yeah, right. Smith didn't just say that. I didn't just hear that. I'm reaching for the phone to schedule a hearing test."

This was unthinkable!

Smith cleared his throat, smiled, looked at the floor briefly to gather himself, and then went back on the attack. One more college try.

"J, do you know what the South's fight song is?"

"No, can't say that I do."

"My uncle went there for a couple of years and he would chant it at every family gathering trying to humor us. It's pretty catchy:

> *Rip 'em up, tear 'em up, leave 'em in the lurch.*
> *Down with the heathen, up with the church!*

"Jobab, you want to hear that in your ears on Saturday afternoons, or *Rammer Jammer!*"

Smith meant it as a sneer, an insult, revealing this juvenile poem from the previous century that you might expect from folks who were either not very sensitive, or at the least not interested in football. Sort of like, you want to go play for a school that thinks football is a joke?

"I get the church part," J said quietly, undaunted. "They are an Episcopal school. It's all meant in fun. They know they will never be great again—they aren't even trying to be great in football. They could, but never would, re-enter the SEC. They have moved on. Their 13,000 acre campus is a haven of study and academics, and the athletics are for students who need an outlet. Though on a very small scale, their athletics do give the school a rallying point. I get it."

I watched in awe. I couldn't believe what was transpiring. Here was my friend, Jobab Robinson, he of rare football ability, even rarer brain, and world-class speed even though yet a teenager, basically telling the University of Alabama Crimson Tide assistant football coach, don't call me, I'll call you. I'm headed the opposite direction, in more ways than one, from Tuscaloosa.

Recruiter Smith muttered, "Well, I'll sewanee." And with that, he got up and excused himself.

He would be back. But he would need some new ammunition.

8

The Church Volcano

In addition to all things football, church life was a major feature of our lives. We went Sunday mornings to Sunday School and preaching service, and then that afternoon to youth group, and Sunday evening service. There was Wednesday night prayer meeting (which meant that we didn't practice Little League baseball or youth football on Wednesday nights). We had covered dish church potluck dinners, Christmas bazaars, and youth camps. Our friends all went to church and it was just a normal part of life.

We cycled through preachers on a regular basis at Sugar Hill Methodist. Something about, "The bishop moves them around." I wasn't quite sure how all that worked, but every few years, the old guy would move out of a house called the parsonage and a new one would move in. I especially liked the ones who had kids my age.

I didn't realize when I was younger that we expected a lot of these men of God. They were supposed to care for the sick and dying. Help us through our life's challenges. Keep the church in order and the collections coming in and being counted. They spoke to us often, and we expected them to be witty, clever, and great communicators. And if they happened to be that on one Sunday, we expected at least the same the next week. I did, however, *pity the poor preacher who tried to bring the Good News of Everlasting Life on a weekend in which both Auburn and Alabama lost.* The dejection of the parishioners cannot be overcome in a single hour on a Sunday morning. The pall was so thick on those rare Sundays after the previous day's double loss, I wondered why even go to church? No one is going to feel like getting into it. But off we trudged, hoping for better things next Saturday.

Our church was a fixture in the community. We were a solid presence, not as large as First Baptist, but larger than the Presbyterians, and larger than at least one other Baptist church, which went by the name of Victory. More on that church a bit later.

Actually, my advanced education into all things Alabama football took place at church one memorable Sunday night. Back in early December of 1972, the Methodists were having their annual church business meeting called a Charge Conference. The finance chairman was John Ed Mackay, who had graduated from Auburn in 1957, the only year up until that time Auburn had won a national championship. The Administrative Board chairman was Peter Martin, a business school graduate from Alabama. He had been encouraged to go to Bama by a second cousin of Joe Willie Namath himself. He was a nice enough fellow but did seem a little tense at times. But that probably coincided with his businesslike attitude, worrying about the details just a bit too much. Seems that sort of went with the engrossed businessman side of him.

Well, this church meeting was just a few days after Auburn had blocked two Alabama punts in the final six minutes from almost the exact same spot on the field and David Langer had run them both in for touchdowns and Auburn had won the Iron Bowl 17-16. When it came time for

John Ed's report to the Conference, he cheerily said, "Looks like our financial picture is super, and we will definitely finish the year in the black with a resounding financial victory especially considering where we were this time last year...We are headed that way unless, of course, something unexpected and stupid happens, like two blocked punts in the final six minutes! All I can say is, let's hope we don't 'Punt, Bama, Punt'." With a playful grin, he was quite proud of himself for his communication framing and wit. John Ed sat down.

Snickers were heard throughout the audience from Auburn fans, while Tide fans generally grimaced and groaned, no doubt expecting such banter to follow them many days afterwards. This was a first fruits of the torturous memory that would never be erased. It just went with the Iron Bowl territory.

However, when the noise stopped, all eyes turned to Peter, the chairman. His eyes were fixated on the piece of paper holding the agenda. At first, he was totally immovable but then his knuckles which were gripping his pencil turned white and his jaw clenched. He was waiting for the moment to pass, and ready to ask if there were any pertinent questions on the aforementioned financial report, but then someone laughed out loud, reliving the impossible Auburn comeback, and John Ed smiled and triumphantly laughed even harder, no doubt reveling in his own wit once again.

That's when the eruption occurred.

Peter jumped up in a rage and threw a right jab that landed squarely on John Ed's jaw. The breaking of bones was loud enough that Mrs. Murphy sitting in the back of the room heard it. She fainted.

Folks rushed to restrain Peter, while others attended to John Ed's physical needs, including one who quickly ran to the church office for a telephone and called an ambulance.

For the record, the church charge conference was terminated at that point.

The next week, 35 members signed a petition asking Peter to apologize. He refused, wanting John Ed to do so first. John Ed was in no mood to apologize for what he thought was a good-natured barb, and simply part of the statewide football culture. Besides, *he* was the victim of physical violence. Why should *he* apologize?

It really got ugly, though, when Peter immediately decided to leave Sugar Hill Methodist and go form a Baptist church. He took 12 people with him, all of whom thought John Ed's "playful barb" was over the line. No one noticed at first, but the 35 who signed the petition asking for apology were all Auburn fans. The 12 who left were graduates of Tuscaloosa. They went and formed Victory Baptist, a name which was subject to various rounds of speculation as to why it was chosen. Maybe the Tiders were free of those Auburn fans, and that was the victory they were hoping for? Or maybe the title was just a reflection of what usually happens when Bama plays. Bama gets the win.

However, it wasn't known till some time later that the real reason Peter had exploded like he did was that his frustration had boiled over in regards to a bet on that game he had made with his Uncle Donald for $300. Even though Bama was heavily favored, Donald had bragged so loud and long about Auburn that Peter had told him to put up or shut up. Donald took him up on it quickly, saying he "just had that feeling." As soon as the Tigers won, he called Peter and asked him what time he could collect. And he would appreciate having it in new, crisp $50 bills. Peter was so distraught he didn't answer him but just put down the phone on the table and walked away. His wife said later he had seemed disoriented, like he had gotten news that a relative had suddenly died who was supposedly in good health. All of that would surely add up as to why zeal for the Tide turned to physical explosion.

This story about the founding of Victory Baptist Church left an indelible mark on me—was I to expect such behavior throughout my lifetime if the Iron Bowl didn't turn out so well? Would the reminder of the loss of a football game lead to blows—in church, no less—between two men who had absolutely zero influence on the outcome of the game?

Heaven help us.

9

The Preacher's Dilemma

Pastor Robertson had been at Sugar Hill Methodist about 2 years. He had moved down from New Hampshire where he'd had a fairly successful ministry. He was a good preacher, and the older folks especially liked the way he visited the sick and acknowledged everyone's birthday with a card. But being from up north, he just had not understood Alabamians' passion for college football. He had tried to step in to calm things down when John Ed and Peter had it out during the Charge Conference, but he was not able to referee. The violence was spontaneous and he had not been prepared for such a display of football fandom. He did his pastoral duty and accompanied the ambulance to the hospital, but that was about all the help he could give.

The pastor had learned to eat grits, drink sweet iced tea, make homemade ice cream, and even talk with a slight drawl. But for all of his increasing acculturation, it was abundantly clear that he didn't know how to tolerate Alabama's love for football, and his lack of patience finally got the best of him. (I note that he didn't help himself with the occasional mention of THE Ohio State University, where apparently his uncle had played. Who in Alabama loved or respected the Buckeyes? I didn't know anybody. They might as well have been a team from outer space.) The fact which he couldn't deny was that he was from up north, and that was different.

Daddy talked about the time he had visited his cousin Henry at Harvard, which was up north. (He was never sure how Henry got in to Harvard, but he did, and so we reckoned in the end that was all that mattered.) Anyway, while he was there, he and Henry went to the Harvard-Columbia game at grand old Memorial Stadium in Cambridge. He got there an hour before the kickoff and there were barely 100 people there. Heck, daddy went to the Auburn-Tennessee game at Legion Field in Birmingham one year. He got there an hour before kickoff and he said he could barely find his seat, it was so crowded with 70,000 plus screaming maniacs. He noted that dozens of people had arrived at least by Wednesday in their RVs, to camp out and get in position. I mean after all, it was Auburn football. And no one wanted to be late to the date. You'd better find your seat, early. Or you might not.

This was the environment into which Pastor Robertson landed. Rabid fans. Their love of football dominated life.

He had noticed that he found it easy to preach on Sundays after Auburn and Alabama had both won the previous day. The congregants seemed lively, attentive, and lighthearted. But let one or the other team lose on the previous Saturday—or heaven forbid!—*both* teams lose on the same weekend, and the preacher might as well cut it short and go to the restaurant early and convene the BBR club, or Beat the Baptists to the Restaurant. *Feeling spiritual just wasn't on the agenda that day.* There was the occasional odd person who didn't seem to really care who won, but they were so different that people didn't pay them much attention. A true Alabamian would care, and would take it personally if their team failed to beat their SEC rival just a few hours before. Feeble attempts to explain why they lost clouded their reason and inhibited their worship. Maybe college football affection really was something like a religion.

Football loyalty affected one's heart, one's entire being. And wasn't that the place where worship came from? I heard about a true blue Auburn fan over at Brundidge named Slim Harris who was so distraught after Auburn lost three straight to start one season, he didn't kiss his wife for a month. His hormones were totally shattered. How could he think about love in the midst of something that felt like a natural disaster? For church parishioners, the parallel was true: how could they worship if they were in a shattered state?

Pastor Robertson decided to meet this silly dilemma head on. There was no reason for the people of God to be so consumed with just a game. They were there to worship, and they must do so wholeheartedly, notwithstanding who won yesterday's football game. It was time to take action. He was the shepherd, and it was obvious the sheep needed some direction. So one Sunday Pastor Robertson bravely announced, "I understand that the Crimson Tide lost a big game yesterday…"

Before he could make his point, he received an immediate verbal barrage back from a Joe Lester, who just happened that weekend to be visiting his Aunt Ruby. Joe was a generally pleasant, middle-aged person, who came to town a few times a year, but as the folks around Sugar Hill would say, he "wasn't quite right." He was openly agitated at the reminder of the Tide's defeat. He suddenly grumbled loud enough for everyone to hear, "They wouldn't have lost if they had a decent quarterback."

"That's right!" someone else piped up. Many nods greeted this second to the motion.

Pastor Robertson had always heard that hecklers would enliven most sermons but this was on the verge of getting out of hand real fast, particularly as it was clear that everyone was awake and listening. He realized he had not been taught in seminary how to face church eruptions built around college football loyalties. So, he chose the path of pretending that he hadn't heard them, but without much success as the congregation was suddenly agitated at the open reminder of the Crimson Tide's untimely and unexpected defeat. Mentioning the Bama loss elicits a response which is more like grabbing a person on a severely sunburned shoulder, rather than being praised for demonstrating wisdom and pastoral acumen.

Though visibly shaken, Pastor Robertson tried to press on.

"I've noticed that people take their football so seriously that when their team loses on Saturday, they are dragging on Sunday, and have a hard time worshipping our Lord..."

Before he could continue his carefully planned persuasive theological point, Joe Lester spoke up again.

"I *said*, if we had a quarterback, we would have won. We had Georgia Tech sucking for air and let them out. Dumb, dumb, dumb!"

Pastor Robertson was immediately overcome with a feeling of being stuck, sort of like sitting in a broken-down Buick at a busy intersection during rush hour and at least five cars are honking at you simultaneously. You want to get the car out of the way but you are helpless to move it by yourself. It was obvious he would need some assistance. He couldn't exactly descend from the pulpit and forcibly remove Joe Lester, nor did he feel it appropriate to address Aunt Ruby from the pulpit and ask her to take him out. The easiest thing, of course, would be for Aunt Ruby to recognize the disturbance and take Joe to the foyer until he calmed down. But she just sat there with a stone face waiting for the pastor to make his response. Or, perhaps a better description would be she was waiting to see how he would get out of this one. Secretly she agreed with Joe but she didn't say anything. It was clear to her that Bama definitely needed a quarterback.

Pastor Robertson bravely (or stupidly, depending on your perspective) continued: "I'm hoping that we can work through this. I don't want our devotion to the Lord on Sunday to depend on who wins the game on Saturday. After a lot of thought and prayer, I've decided that what we need to do is..."

Before he could proceed with the announcement of his brilliant plan, he was suddenly interrupted by the chairman of the administrative board. "Preacher, that's how it is. They need a quarterback."

Pastor Robertson fumbled through his mental filing cabinet, looking for any notes or conversations from seminary as to how to address this unfolding dilemma. The crowd was getting out of hand. Mob violence in a church meeting is not a pleasant sight. He had already witnessed that at the church business meeting which did not end well.

Passion for Alabama football was taking over the place. These Alabama folks weren't budging. This northern boy would have to figure out how to work within an environment that bled certain colors. Or, it was going to be a short-lived ministry in the Deep South.

Which it was. Within four months, he had retreated to New Hampshire, just before the Bama and Auburn spring football games.

Tucked away in the woods of New Hampshire, it was told that he found preaching a lot easier on Sundays. Autumn Saturdays up there didn't seem to affect his effort at sacred communication. I guess folks had other things to worry about. He was back in the land of the Ivy League's Dartmouth College. They played Brown, Harvard, Yale and Princeton. Hardly anyone noticed. Or cared.

And the recap of those games never interrupted another of his sermons.

10

The Barbershop

I went to church every Sunday, and City Barber every Saturday. I'm sure I needed to go to church. However, I got a weekly haircut whether I needed it or not. Visits to City Barber were an integral part of my growing-up years.

The establishment was located in the center of town, both literally and figuratively. Right at the corner of 1st and Main, it had been in downtown Sugar Hill for as long as anyone could remember. Easy to find, convenient to spend time in. Not out of the way to anywhere. On your way to the county courthouse? Then why not stop in when you finish with your business. Planning a lunch break at Clara's Diner? City Barber is right next door. And the gentlemen who frequented the place had the pipeline to all the information that was of relevance to the community. If they didn't know about it, it probably wasn't worth talking about. Pick a subject: politics, finance, religion (including their perspective on fights in the church business meeting), newcomers, weather, or football. The boys of City Barber knew about it, and loved to tell the story.

Adding to the southern charm of the place was Mr. Leroy Smithson. He was an older black gentleman who manned the shoe shine corner of City Barber. Either before or after the hair-cutting, Mr. Leroy worked his magic on the foot leather of the clients. I never remember him saying much. He was usually reading the paper when he wasn't engaged in shining, or when he was working, he was focused in concentration, leaving no detail untouched as it related to his chosen profession. He was the shoe shine expert in town. In fact, he was the one the family had hired to polish to perfection the shoes that were on Old Man Parker in his casket.

Another thing Mr. Leroy was known for was a side hobby of his: he opened Coke bottles with his teeth. He did it without a set fee, but the boys of City Barber usually paid him a quarter, or "two bits" as the old timers classified that sum of money. They would hoot and cackle when he did it, and then usually tip him an extra quarter after he handed over the now open bottle. Everybody loved Mr. Leroy, and the display of his gift was just another part of the entertainment. (I spent my childhood wondering how those metal bottle caps didn't break his teeth or injure his gums, but he never seemed to have any problems.)

Sometimes, hair-cutting in the Fall was particularly challenging. TV reception could be a bit hazy with the old rabbit ears antenna. The channels carrying the Tide or Tigers might not come in to the satisfaction of the clientele, and they would invariably grumble, fold up their ever-present *Montgomery Advertiser* newspaper, and file out, uttering their goodbyes and see-ya-laters. They had to find a decent TV.

It wasn't any easier on the owner, Ronnie Thompkins. He wanted to watch the game as badly as the next guy, but he knew he needed to pay attention to hairlines, ear hairs, and eye brows, or he would be toast. A good man's haircut didn't get noticed as much as a bad one, which was significant, unwanted, negative advertising.

Apart from judgment on his barbering skills, Mr. Ronnie, as he was called, was negatively discussed for a suspicious absence one year on the third Saturday in October. (Everyone knew that Alabama played Tennessee on the third Saturday in October, and up until that time, had done so for more than 50 years.) Mr. Ronnie had a sign on the door one third October Saturday which simply read, "The Proprietor of City Barber regrets that he is sick today. He hopes to be back on Monday afternoon."

He escaped detection until a nephew of City Barber regular Peter Benson happened to stop in at a bar in Possum Ridge, about 30 miles away, and there was Mr. Ronnie, big as life, sitting at the bar watching the Bama-UT game. When reported back through the family channels—not intentionally, but one of those, "Oh by the way, interestingly, I was in Possum Ridge last Saturday, and guess who I saw?"—Mr. Ronnie firmly denied it, and swore it had to be his look-alike. Case closed from his perspective, as he swore, again, that he was in bed with the flu. (And he was fully recovered by Monday afternoon.)

Mr. Ronnie always closed City Barber on Monday mornings because he ate so much one Sunday night at the Methodist Church covered dish fried chicken dinner that he slept in on Monday morning. He realized right then how nice that was after a long weekend. So, he closed City Barber until 1:30 on Monday afternoons, and his customers knew it and didn't complain. They planned around it, and in the autumns, saved their football commentaries of the previous Saturday for that time slot.

Since I attended City Barber every Saturday, it held a firm place in my growing up years. The sights and smells were iconic, and stayed with me for years: hair tonic being forced out of its bottle by slapping and prodding; Mr. Ronnie sharpening his straight blade razor on a leather strap, back and forth, back and forth, back and forth, doing so till it was sharp enough to cut through the hide of a feral hog; the dull, quiet roar of the electric razor on the neck, trimming those neck hairs just before the removal swish of the white sheet guarding the upper body from fallen hair, and application of talcum powder for reasons I didn't understand; the gentle push of the broom, sweeping up hair; Mr. Leroy furiously wrapping his cloth around the back of the customer's shoes right at the end of the shining.

Hair cutting was the reason for City Barber's existence. But several men gathered day after day just to talk and tell stories. They didn't go to get their hair cut. It was their social connecting point. They told the same stories over and over. Each time the stories were met by knee-slapping and howls and laughter like the inhabitants of City Barber had never heard them before. They talked about Tommy Lewis coming off the sidelines to make the tackle, and they would alternate between laughter ("The old Rice boys didn't see that coming!") and pride ("Tommy just couldn't help it; he was just *too full of Alabama!*") One of the regulars at City Barber had actually been at the Cotton Bowl in Dallas on that fateful New Year's Day, and his presence made the story even more real and more powerful. Particularly poignant was how he spoke of the collective gasp from the crowd when they saw Tommy jump into the field of play and stop cold Dicky Moegle on his breakaway run.

Another of the favorite stories told at City Barber had to do with an unplanned Sunday morning football practice. Alabama had failed the previous day to annihilate some hapless opponent like Ole Miss. They had squeaked by with just a few points' victory and so Coach Bryant announced that due to their sloppiness and embarrassing performance they would have practice at 5:30 the next morning, which of course was Sunday. So, the Crimson Tide showed up, and Bear informed the team that he had notified his preacher that he would not be there that day, and then he commenced to put them through you-know-what. About 8:30, Bear announced "Alright, all you Christian boys can go on and shower and get ready for Sunday School and church. The rest of us are going to stay out here and practice." As the story goes, *right then there was a mass conversion to Christianity.* Even though the regulars had heard the story many times, the whole barber shop crowd would hoot and holler, particularly if there just happened to be one among them who didn't know it. Then after the laughter played out, they would quietly shake their heads, marveling at the dedication of Coach Bryant to mold a winner. That was college football in the great state of Alabama—their teams won because they did some mysterious thing called "wanting it." I wasn't exactly sure what "wanting it" or "wanting it bad enough" was, but it was what I was supposed to do when I played.

Someone would follow with a reminder of how when Coach Bryant started at Texas A&M, he took two busloads of football players to a summer camp at some place in the deserted countryside called Junction City. Story goes that practice and drills and adapting to Bear's ways were so brutal that they only needed to go back home in one bus. The equivalent of one busload had deserted the Bear and blended into the Texas landscape, many at night, hitchhiking or taking a commercial bus out of there. I reckon they found out they just didn't 'want it' bad enough.

The story I remember the most from City Barber was not funny.

One day, just as Mr. Ronnie was deftly snipping the hair around the top of my ears, someone said, "Did you boys go to Old Man Parker's funeral? I thought it was a real good service."

Johnny Morris piped up, "Yep, it was. Real sweet. And he looked real good in the casket. Charley did a good job on him." (I wasn't sure how you made a dead man look good, but I kept listening.) "Hey, did anyone ever say how he died? I don't remember the cause of death being stated in the obituary section in the *Advertiser*."

"Naw, never did hear. Did any of you boys?"

For some reason at this point, Mr. Ronnie slightly, but noticeably, exhaled. While a small chorus in unison of grunts and head-shaking was going on, one of the regulars noticed that Ronnie had stopped cutting my hair and acted like he knew something.

"Ronnie, do you know? Did you hear anything? City Barber is the place for sharing such local knowledge. What'd you hear?"

At this point, my $1.25 haircut was grinding to a halt. Ronnie cleared his throat and leaned back on the counter, and said, "Well, as a matter of fact, I did hear. It had to do with news from Alexander Smith."

"Alexander Smith!" Johnny Morris bellowed. "You mean the number one poker player in north Alabama? That no-good Alexander Smith?"

"Yes sir, one and the same."

"Well, Ronnie, how did he know?"

Ronnie again hesitated. His breathing was labored. The continuation of my hair cut was now a hopeless proposition. And with Mr. Ronnie visibly shaken, I sure didn't mind if he wasn't wielding that straight-edge razor on a part of me that could do some serious long-term damage with a slip of the hand.

He swallowed hard, and figured he might as well let out the news. The boys were bound to find out sometime. I noticed two of them stopped reading their papers, and leaned forward.

"Smith came in here a few days ago. Seems that Old Man Parker had bet $500 on the Iron Bowl. Punt, Bama, Punt, and all that, and Auburn surprised everybody with a big win. So, Parker ended up in a poker game in a house near the Tennessee line, intending to win back his money. They smoked, drank, and played poker well into the night, and it wasn't going good for him. He lost all his money. Alexander Smith made sure of that. Bad draws of the hand combined with Smith's expertise and the next thing you know, Old Man Parker went broke. Seems Parker had handed over his football betting losses without his wife finding out. Now, he was trying to sneak the money back into the cookie jar before she discovered it missing. But, as I said, he doubled his problem when he lost another $500.

"About midnight, Old Man Parker thought of a way to restore some of his lost honor, even if he was broke. So he dramatically straggled to his feet, and announced, 'I swear by the grave of Bear Bryant...'

"That was met by a bunch of resistance. 'Oh c'mon on, Parker, don't be serious! You don't mean that.' And 'Parker, don't say something you gonna regret. You know that's not a good thing to say.'"

I had grown up in a world of various Southern superstitions, like making an 'x' on the windshield if a black cat ran across the road. But I had never heard of swearing on a dead man's grave. It sounded serious.

"Leave me be, boys. I swear by the grave of Bear Bryant that I if I lose the next hand...I'm gonna drink me 12 Budweisers in a row. You can't have my money, 'cause you already have all that. You don't want my clothes—this ain't some cheap game of strip poker, and besides that, they stink. Ha! No sir, I'm going to submit to consecutive beer guzzling. But if I win, you boys are gonna send me home with two cases of Budweiser. Deal?!"

"They continued to try to talk him out of it, but he wouldn't be persuaded. He held up his hands, persisted and then said, "Look, anyone here doesn't like it, they can hold their nose and go down to the bottom of Guntersville Lake for all I care. You think I care?! I really don't. *Deal me in, boys, I'm feeling lucky, punk!*"

"So they did. On his first draw, as the story goes, he got terrible cards. Threw in two, drew two. Still terrible. Not long thereafter, Parker folded.

"Alright boys, I swore on the grave of Bear Bryant, and I'll do what I said. Bring me the Buds!"

"He popped the top on the first one and announced to Smith, 'This Bud's for you!' He downed it, with a goofy grin. He wobbled again, but then he popped another, and finished it off. Then a third.

"He popped the top on the fourth, took one swig, gasped and spewed, his eyes rolled back in his head, and he collapsed backwards like a 50 pound bag of flour. His head hit the concrete floor with a sickening, mighty thud, and blood started oozing out. Someone hollered to call an ambulance. Someone else said, "Does anybody know CPR? We've got a problem here!"

"Nobody knew CPR. Not sure it would have helped if they had. When the ambulance crew arrived, they checked him out, and didn't even work on him, but announced that he was dead.

"The coroner showed up, and started his analysis, talked to the card players (at least those who were left; some had fled the scene due to the quasi-illegal and murky nature of the game in that part of Alabama), and determined that Old Man Parker had died of a heart attack. The blow to the head might have contributed to his demise, but the coroner said he was probably dead when he hit the floor."

City Barber got quiet. The only sounds heard were those outside the shop, of the occasional car horn, folks hollering at each other down the street, and some big birds bouncing around, playing outside the plate glass window. Mr. Ronnie seemed relieved. It was like he had been carrying this awful news on his chest, and needed to get rid of it, but hadn't had the opportunity. I noticed Mr. Leroy just staring out the window from his perch on the shoe shine stand, doing so without expression.

Finally, Milt Patterson spoke up. "What a way to go! I didn't even know Parker was a beer drinker. I knew he ran around with some beer-drinking buddies, but not him! I mean I knew he took a swig now and then, but I thought he was mostly just friends with those kinds of guys. Wasn't he a member of the Baptist church for like 30 or 40 years?"

"Fifty-two," someone offered.

"Fifty-two! The very mischief. He was a deacon, for what, 20 of those?"

"Thirty-five, at least."

"Fifty-two years in church, and 35 as a deacon! Who knew he had these problems?"

"His wife did, but never told anybody. Didn't want to damage his reputation. Can't say that I blame her."

My haircut resumed. I hadn't really needed one anyway, but it was Saturday, and I had dutifully trooped off to get one. Mr. Ronnie finished me up quickly, dusted off my hair-cutting sheet, then took my money without saying a word.

As I got out of the chair, I looked around the room at a bunch of stunned old-timers. One of their ranks had fallen, and they weren't sure how to process it. Time would only tell if the revelation of Old Man Parker's demise would sully the reputation of the biggest Tide fan anyone had ever known.

At the least, I would know the reason for his funeral: loyalty to the Crimson Tide and betting on their unending success "had done him in," as they say.

It became clearer to me as I grew up that college football was some kind of life or death proposition for a whole bunch of folks.

Literally.

11

The Wedding

I'm happy to record that in my youth I only attended one wedding. One was plenty.

My Uncle Louie, on my daddy's side, remarried after his wife, Ermaline, was run over by a postal truck on Rural Route 6 in Marengo County. He had moved to Wetumpka and met a lady at work and they were ready to tie the knot. I was actually invited, or more correctly termed 'volunteered' by my mother, to be in the wedding party, as an usher. However, I was so unfamiliar with all things wedding-related, I thought that wedding party meant a *party*. Made sense to me. People who got married seemed to be happy, so we should all join in with a party, and a celebration. You know, the kind with punch and cookies and games.

It was a rude awakening that being in the wedding party meant that I had to dress up in a starchy shirt, wear a suit all day that was too small for me (it had been a while since my parents had invested in a new one, as my old one had been overtaken by my growth spurt), slick my hair, and basically take instructions on how to walk older ladies down the aisle to their seats. That activity was intermingled with passing out printed programs of the upcoming service, set against a backdrop of what seemed to me to be repetitive, dreary organ music.

This was not the way I had wanted to spend a prime Saturday in October. There were only four of them, maybe five, and we were burning one inside a church doing something, which best I could tell, could be handled on a different day. This just wasn't right. I had thought I was going to a party. But I ended up trapped, like in a prison. There was no way out until I had paid my debt to society.

I heard that Uncle Louie's new wife was from Minnesota, and thus an immigrant to the land of Dixie. I could not recall ever hearing anything about the passion or greatness of college football in the state of Minnesota. If they had it, they must have kept it to themselves. We sure didn't know about it. Why, I had never heard of them playing in the Cotton or Sugar Bowls. Were we sure they had a team?

That would explain why she reportedly insisted on getting married on an October Saturday. Uncle Louie had advised her that as far as his side of the family was concerned, that was a bad idea; folks were traveling to wherever the Tide or Tigers were playing. She scoffed at that, saying that of course friends and family would show up for his wedding. A wedding is not a usual occurrence. Football happens every Saturday in the fall. Surely, she said, for the purpose of witnessing the public exchange of blessed nuptials till death do us part, they will forgo *one* of those silly games (yes, I heard that she had used the word 'silly').

Wrong. The wedding planner had pleaded with them to pick a different day in a different season. Common to all successful wedding planners in Alabama, she was equipped with football schedules. She knew that folks had priorities, and when those priorities were made known, the hard truth often came out front and center: "Congratulations on your upcoming wedding! Sorry we can't attend. *We have a long-standing obligation on that day.* We will send a gift, and can't wait to see the pictures. So glad for y'all! Love, so and so."

Sure enough, the crowd was sparse, mostly attended by folks that I had not recognized as known for being particularly energetic football fans. No doubt, they had a team preference, but they weren't really involved in football, so they showed up at the church. About 20 of them.

As I was walking one of the grandfathers and his wife down the aisle to their seats, I noticed that he had something in his ear. I didn't get a good look at it, as I was trying to make sure that I led them to the proper pew, so I kept my eyes focused forward. But after I deposited them to their prime seating, as I had been instructed, I turned to leave and discerned that whatever was sticking in grandpa's ear, was attached to a wire. Must have been one of those fancy hearing aids. They say that older people often need help with their hearing. And for sure he wanted to hear all that was happening at this fine event.

Having never been to a wedding before, I wasn't sure what to expect with the sequential steps, but all of a sudden, about 7 minutes past the appointed hour, the vestibule of the church got very busy. Down at the altar waiting on the bride were the preacher, Uncle Louie, and his two friends standing up to support him (one of whom had tickets to the Bama-Mississippi State game that day, and who was not impressed with the wedding scheduling). There they stood in their finery waiting on the bridal party. (There's that word again. I never remembered folks looking so nervous at a party in all my life.) The organist hit the deep-throated notes, or whatever you call them, and that was the cue for the bride's two assistants to march down one after the other with flowers in hand.

I was amazed by what I was watching in the back of the church. The bride was in a huge white dress with the back sticking out (I learned later they called that a 'train', for some reason), and two different ladies were touching her face and clothes and fawning over her to make sure everything was in place, including her hair which was coiffed to the max. And it was big hair. As the saying goes, the bigger the hair, the closer to God. However, my observation was that she didn't look like a woman who had God on her mind at that moment. She looked nervous as a cat. So did her handlers. I was nervous just watching.

Then her uncle, filling in for her deceased father, hooked his arm in hers and led her away to the altar. On a mighty signal from the organ, and the preacher's upraised hand, the crowd stood all at once, with folks turning and craning their heads to the back of the sanctuary. Down the aisle she went, headed to the altar, in the midst of smiles and stares.

That's when it got really interesting.

When they arrived at the altar, the organist let go of the chord she was playing, and the preacher began. "Dearly beloved, we are gathered here today…" But something wasn't right. There was some noise interference.

I had turned towards the general direction of the unknown source of noise, when I heard a distinctive and familiar voice, which was shouting, "Touchdown Auburrrrrnnnnnn!" And then the voice said, "Take that,

Tennessee! Tigers back on top! Goodness gracious! Andrews went in untouched from the 20."

I instinctively looked at the preacher, who I will add, was not amused. The wedding party at the front of the church was alternating between laughter and looks of horror.

They were all staring in the direction of the grandfather that I had escorted to his pew.

Turns out that the contraption in his ear was not a hearing aid. It was an audio ear piece connected by wire to a transistor radio which was clipped on to his belt, hidden under his coat. When the congregation had stood to acknowledge the entrance of the bride, he must have inadvertently pulled on the wire and dislodged the ear piece connection from the radio. So, instead of privately enjoying the Auburn play-by-play, the radio was on full bore and heard by all throughout the church. The volume was high, as he was hard of hearing.

Two ladies in the vestibule seemed close to experiencing heart attacks. One suddenly pushed me in the back and commanded, "Go get that radio!"

What was I supposed to do? I was a teenage boy, attending my first wedding, and they were trying to thrust me forward as an untrained, junior policeman to apprehend the offending citizen. I was supposed to go to the second pew on the left, right in front of the bride, and command a 70-something year old grandpa to hand over the contraband? Wouldn't his beloved wife poke him in the ribs and tell him to turn it off? That would be easy, right? Then we could get on with the show. It was embarrassing, but they could turn off the radio, and then we would keep moving.

Well, grandma was even more deaf than he was, but she didn't let on to that fact. During the chaos, she kept staring straight ahead, oblivious to the reason for the finger-pointing and scowls that were laser-focused in their direction.

The noise and roar from Jordan-Hare Stadium were distinctive. They overtook the wedding. The bride started crying. Her attendants tried to comfort her, instinctively looking around for tissues. Before I could make my move (and if I had made it, it would have been a reluctant move), the preacher addressed grandpa and asked him to turn it off.

"Huh?" Grandpa said.

"Turn off your radio, please."

"My what?"

The game was in a commercial break after the Auburn touchdown, now on to an ad for Goody's Headache Powders.

Goody's could have made a fortune if they had been present with a sales booth at the wedding.

"Your radio!" The preacher repeated more loudly. The Reverend pointed to grandpa's belt. He looked down. He first fumbled to reconnect the wire, but was unsuccessful. Then his wife leaned over, having realized that the reason for this interruption to the wedding program was based on her husband's technical gaffe. She grabbed the radio and tried to turn it off. But things got worse.

Instead of rotating the little dial to the off position, she went the wrong direction and turned it up even louder. I didn't think it was possible to get louder, but it was. The

Jordan-Hare stadium noise increased, while the Auburn announcer's exuberance hit new heights, as the hated Tennessee Vols were on their way to defeat.

Grandma reversed her course and the dial landed in the off-position. Then there was an eerie, uncomfortable sort of silence. How do you move on from that?

The offending twosome kept looking straight ahead. Grandma straightened her dress, pulling it down around her mid-section, and nervously, fixed her hair. Grandpa's face was expressionless. If there was any hint of remorse, it was probably related to the fact that he would not get to hear the rest of the Auburn game.

After glaring at grandpa, the preacher broke the awkward silence. He turned to the bride.

"Miss, on behalf of all here, I apologize for this unfortunate interruption. No one should be subjected to such an intrusion. Please, we ask for your forgiveness."

He could have left it there, and gone back on script, but he paused, and unwisely chose humor to try to soothe the wounds. "Now that we all know the Auburn-Tennessee score, we will proceed."

I thought it was funny, but the deafening lack of laughter, or giggles, told me otherwise.

Nothing but crickets.

The ceremony proceeded, and we limped to the finish. When it was over, the couple recessed, and the bride had at least a slight smile. I noticed that she had not even looked in grandpa's direction on the way up the aisle to the vestibule.

I learned an important lesson that day, a life-lesson worth keeping at this, my first wedding: Joe Billy, if you ever decide to get married, do not get married in Alabama during football season.

At least, not on a Saturday.

Part Two:

Roll Tide

12

The Plainsman

No big surprise, but I attended college at Auburn, enrolling 2 months shy of my 18th birthday. Daddy had said he would send me to college, and gladly pay my way. But there was only one choice of school. It sure wasn't Bama, Ole Miss, or Tennessee (which he seemed to loathe almost as much as Bama). "Enjoy your college education!"—as long as it is on the plains of east Alabama. I shrugged and said, sure, why not. Plenty of friends were going there, and we would learn the next chapter of life together. We figured out studying (which I had done very little of at Sugar Hill High School), meals, laundry, shopping, spending money, trips home on the holidays, and changing sheets on my bed (at least once per quarter was the plan, maybe more often; I would have to see how the mood struck me).

Some had figured out fraternities, like Kappa Alpha or Lambda Chi, and did something called "pledged" (which I guess meant pledged their loyalty—and their finances) but that wasn't me. I just wasn't that sociable. Nor did I have much disposable income. I was doing good just to go to college. If I had any extra, discretionary money to be used, and that a benevolent gift from daddy, or my grandmother who occasionally wrote to me and sent me a check, it probably wouldn't find its way into a fraternity's treasury.

The fraternity brothers did have their own houses, which would have provided some kind of conveniences, a more residential feeling, and built-in brotherhood, but I was a dormitory guy. That's what I could afford, and that's where I stayed. I couldn't have everything.

My first dorm roommate, Chester, was from a small west Alabama town. There were two things about him that I remember: one is that he showed up with a fire in his belly for the Auburn Tigers. I thought of him as almost a miniature Uncle Moon Pie. And secondly, he had a girlfriend back home. That was a complicating factor in making the transition to a new life. He had to either go home on the weekends and see her—which he seemed to do quite often—or call her on the pay phone from the dorm lobby. Both of those were expensive propositions twenty years before the end of the 20th century for an unemployed college freshman.

However, I soon went through roommate trauma. West Alabama Girlfriend reportedly dumped him, as he shared with me in tears one night, for reasons still not clear to him. Certainly had something to do with another guy, but he never felt he got the whole story. News of her departure seemed to set off a tiger in him, and he became something of a wild man, a rogue college student trying to leave his mark all around campus. It wasn't pretty to watch.

Chester didn't finish his freshman year. Got a DUI, and spent a night in the Lee County jail. His daddy sent him home, and he got a job in the local hardware store while attending a nearby junior college. He sent me a letter and told me this, also asking for me to send some things left behind in the dorm room after his arrest. I obliged, and spent the rest of the first semester of my freshman year without a roommate.

It had been less than 20 years since Governor Wallace had stood in the doorway at the University of Alabama, pledging to keep it lily white. I would have thought we would have moved on from there, and realized that our racial prejudice was destructive, and wrong. But I experienced it at Auburn, listening to friends tell jokes that were off-color and inappropriate. I watched them draw lines around social circles that didn't include blacks. And generally, with disdain they looked down on blacks, and as they described certain, harmful actions taken towards blacks, and the attitudes behind those cruel acts, they would let it slip in conversation, "that's how we did it back home."

Black athletes, particularly football players, were somewhat admired and in small ways protected from the racism leaks, but the black student population was not treated with the equality and normalcy I expected. I was chagrined at this, and tried to cultivate relationships with black friends. Paul Washington and Jobab Robinson had been two of my closest friends, and I had no reason not to expect that I would have friends at Auburn who were different from me.

As I started my Auburn career, I was determined to attend every home football game, and some on the road, depending on the availability of personal funds, and would maybe get to see Paul Washington on the Crimson Tide offensive unit at Legion Field during the annual Iron Bowl. My numerous and obvious points of athletic lack kept me from any fleeting dreams of a being an Auburn Tiger. I would be an observer, rather than a participant on fall afternoons. I had made peace with this future path despite my starry-eyed childhood ambitions.

Though I was aware that I couldn't cut it on the football field, I did have a gift for writing. Awareness of this led me to a choice of major, and I settled early on Journalism. Daddy drilled into me, and in fact commanded, that I be practical in my decision.

When he left me in front of my freshman dorm, he told me two things: get to heaven, and get a degree you can get a job with. He was right with his direction on both counts. I would continue to follow Jesus Christ, which I had done since I had been a small child, nurtured into the faith at Sugar Hill Methodist. And, I would major in something practical. That meant not majoring in Philosophy, or English, or Mathematics. Turning those study programs into a living wage would require some extra steps educationally, and I was not that interested in further education. I reasoned early on that a four-year's bachelor degree was plenty. I chose Journalism, and I would eventually write for the student newspaper, *The Plainsman.*

As I launched my degree quest, I was able to negotiate the somewhat confusing quad structures at Auburn, and find my way through the intimidating Haley Center, the main classroom building where I took most of my classes. I quickly realized how unprepared I was for college life. I mean, just buying textbooks was an almost overwhelming experience for a new student. While the staff at Auburn's legendary J & M Bookstore softened the pain as much as they could and helped me to find what I needed, still, I had to pay for them. Had never done that before. At Sugar Hill High School, we got assigned textbooks for the semester (complete with doodles and love notes written in the margins from learned ones who had gone before us). The sticker shock of textbook purchases was hard to digest—and explain to my parents.

I don't ever remember taking notes in high school classes. We wrote on handouts, or worksheets, or tests. Or just listened. During lectures at Auburn, people wrote as fast as the wind in spiral notebooks. I wasn't exactly sure what they were writing down and also what they were missing from the lectures as their pen tried to stay in sync with the professor's distribution of wisdom. It was unsettling to me, especially as this note-taking seemed to be part of an expected skill set, and one which I obviously didn't have. But I tried. For the most part, I failed. I learned to listen and try to digest the gist of what the prof was saying.

We knew the teachers at Sugar Hill. We grew up with their children, played Little League baseball with them, and attended Sunday School, and maybe even went on vacation with their families. It was a small town, and we were either personally acquainted, or at least knew of the teachers, and had numerous points of connections with them.

But Auburn was different. Professors came from various backgrounds and profiles, and were all unknown to me. They might as well have been from some far-off place like New York City, for all I knew. Some were talkative and friendly, and were able to boil down for us the great learning we were seeking. They could "put the cookies on a low shelf for us", as one liked to say. But not all were like that.

I had a grumpy freshman English professor. He acted like we were a bother when we asked basic questions which he thought we should know the answers to, but for us, we had not been taught that particular information in high school. We couldn't change that reality.

Another prof, this one who taught writing, used "big words", and when we protested, or asked her to explain, she would shrug, point to the dictionary, and say that college students should know that word. While that kind of response is one approach to pedagogy, it did keep us at arm's length, especially if the classroom was the only place where we saw her. We weren't exactly going on vacation with her family. She sent a strong signal from her responses that she was smarter than we were. We were no match for her mental prowess. We admitted it, we weren't.

But I made it through all the basic classes, even the mathematics ones, somehow. Not with great grades, but they were passable, and I was advancing.

My favorite professor was a Mr. Richards. He had a master's degree in English, and taught American Literature. But he was more at home as a philosopher than a dispenser of the fine points of Lit.

A classic exchange with one of his students illustrated his philosophical bent. I recall that the literature story under class discussion that day had a love theme, involving a spurned lover. Mr. Richards was reflecting on how someone else always wants what you've got. He informed us that, "if you break up with your girlfriend, someone else will want her." One of the young men in the class, who appeared to be on a tormented quest for the meaning of life, and noting how all things seemed to revolve around love, blurted out, "Mr. Richards, what is love?"

Without hesitation, he proclaimed, "Love is when two forces intermingle and coincide with each other, harmoniously. That is love."

That was a big takeaway from my college education.

Another, which also had to do with love, was a revelation that shocked me: I met a number of Auburn co-ed students who were not shy in proclaiming their intention of marriage. The degree they were interested in was something I had never heard of before, but which was talked about widely, and was called the M-R-S degree. I remember that one excitedly said in her junior year that she was so looking forward to her marriage.

So, I asked the logical question, "Who's the lucky guy?"

Her answer left me without response: "I don't know yet, but I am sure that I'll find somebody before the end of my senior year!"

That was a bold statement and reflected a not-too-uncommon mindset. As one of my friends told me in hushed tones one day, "You know, if they don't find a husband at college, where will they? Their odds of success will be severely reduced."

I had never thought of that.

I will admit that this declaration of M-R-S degree-hunting did cause me to look at eligible females with just a little more caution. Could we be friends, and not get on the marriage track together? Could we date, as friends, and call it off if we discovered we were on different pages, relationship-wise?

Apart from the previously-mentioned relationship with Mary Harmon Makowski that didn't survive the best intentions of long-distance love, there were two girls at Auburn that slotted into the category of girlfriend during my time there.

Never mind that I saw a t-shirt one day on campus which read, "Define Girlfriend." Just the mention of that t-shirt opened the door to discussion about boundaries, dating, and latitude for keeping other company. I thought it was funny. Some didn't. I mentioned the t-shirt at a party once, and Shirley Hofzinger said huffily, "We all know what a girlfriend is!" I wondered what her backstory was.

It seemed fairly common that a girlfriend, for the most part, was someone with whom you had taken up steady, or exclusive company. "Going steady" or "going together" seemed to be high school terminology. In college, as we moved towards adulthood, the terminology of boyfriend and girlfriend relationship description was supplemented with "they are together", or "they are an item." Several of my friends made the leap from these various descriptions of girlfriend to fiancé, and we all knew what came after that.

Diane, from Brundidge, Alabama, first caught my eye with her auburn-colored hair. Smart, friendly, and chatty. I loved spending time with her. I went home with her one weekend to meet the parents (an action which seemed to move our relationship to at least signaling a possible different level of interest than just spending time together). Her parents were fun and engaging, and her daddy was outgoing.

But behind that smile, he was protective. As he talked to me about his precious daughter, about whom he let it be known that she was his pride and joy, he would laugh and say that I had better take good care of her, and then he slipped in the classic line, "I've been to prison, and I don't mind going back, if you know what I mean."

I would weakly smile, and mumble, "Yes, sir." I respected him, and he didn't scare me off. Nor did I bother to mention how much time she and I had spent inside my 1968 Ford Galaxie 500 in the far corner of the parking lot, using it as a place to be alone, and talk, and kiss. It probably wasn't worth bringing up.

But after about 8 months of regular dating, Diane got a better offer. A starting inside linebacker spied her in French class one day, made an introductory move, and the next thing I knew, she had gone home with him to Homewood or Hoover or Mountain Brook, or some other fancy Birmingham suburb, to meet the parents.

Yes, they got married her senior year.

The other Auburn co-ed that I fell for was Rachel, from Alex City. She was similar to Diane in some ways, but with one big difference: she was a sorority sister, having pledged to Kappa Delta.

Unlike the frat boys at Auburn, the sorority sisters didn't have their own separate residences. Word around campus was that a wealthy donor had given an enormous financial gift to the university to ensure that they wouldn't. The donor felt that sorority houses would be easily turned into residences of ill repute, and the vulnerable young ladies would not be able to survive the testosterone invasion of the young stallions neighing and racing across the Loveliest Village. So, the semi-defenseless young lass would group with others of her kind, in the same sorority, and live on the same dormitory floor or perhaps find her own apartment.

Thank goodness. At least there she would be safe from male intrusion.

Rachel lived in a dorm, and ate in the cafeteria. I often ate with her, as it was part of my meal plan. We found out that our parents were not happy if we ate out and skipped the "paid-for meals" which were included with our fees. They were sacrificing to send us to this fine establishment of higher education, and they were squeezing every dollar. Taking advantage of all of our advantages was one way to show our gratefulness.

We occasionally went to the Auburn town institution, The Sani-Freeze, or "The Flush", as in Sani-Flush, as it was known, for ice cream. It was across the street from the First Baptist Church. We could go there on Sunday nights to college age Bible study, and then slip over to The Flush for an afterglow event. Actually, it was the epitome of the cheap date. We liked being together, we both liked ice cream, and the price was right. And, one or both of us would usually run into someone we knew. A miniature party developed on the spot. It was a good diversion from the school environment or the class assignments which always seemed to be hanging over our heads back on campus.

My lack of disposable income became a determining factor in the demise of our relationship. Rachel's Kappa Delta social life eventually got the best of me. We liked each other, a lot, and even talked about marriage a time or two. But I couldn't keep up with her fast-paced world, filled with this particular fund-raiser, and that big social fling. And it seemed like they had multiple such events, with mandatory attendance, for every season and for a whole bunch of occasions I couldn't predict. I was more than happy to be her date, but I didn't have the right clothes or the right background for these events in her social circle. I felt increasingly uncomfortable. I just didn't know how to act, nor did I connect with the troop of boy friends who I saw more and more at such events.

Unlike with Diane, who dumped me, I was the one who made the move to tell Rachel that I was backing off, as painful as that was. She cried. I faced the reality that I wasn't interested in being exclusive any longer.

I found out that she soon discovered Mr. Right, who was from out-of-state, and they married one year after graduation. She quickly had twins, her husband passed the bar exam, and life was no doubt good.

Glad she got over me.

War Eagle.

13

The Journalist

Instead of burning up the gridiron of Jordan-Hare stadium, I would write about what I saw, doing so as I mentioned earlier, for the student newspaper. Two weeks into my freshman year, a notice in *The Plainsman* advertised for the equivalent of beat writers for sports who were needed to continue to make the paper a success, and I applied, and got the position. It paid exactly zero, but I did get access to the press box (actually just down the row from the Auburn radio announcers, which to me was pretty heady stuff) and all the free hot dogs, doughnuts and sodas that a college freshman could want, down the hall in the hospitality room for all of us "hard workers." What was not to love about this arrangement? This *quasi* job fit perfectly with my major, and I loved football. So, I was all in. It was a position I held all four years at Auburn.

My *summa* moment, the one that outlasted all others, and which will live in my memory as long as I have my faculties about me, was the day during my senior season of 1982 that Bo Jackson went over the top. Bo reminded me of Jobab Robinson, almost a freak of nature, built physically to perfection. He was not just built, but accompanied by unequaled talent. Subsequently, Bo became the only athlete to ever play in both the NFL and Major League Baseball All-Star games. That lead sentence of his resume is enough to settle most arguments on the greatness of his athletic accomplishments.

Auburn was trailing Bama late in the 4th quarter. Head coach Pat Dye was stymied near the goal line. The Bama defensive line was repelling Auburn's attempt at a late touchdown. Without Auburn penetrating the end zone, the Crimson Tide would win. Not known to any of us observers at the time, Bo convinced Coach Dye to give him the ball, running straight towards the middle of the line of scrimmage, and then he would leave his feet and hurdle over both lines of huge, grunting linemen into the end zone. All were expecting the usual man-on-man tug of war, dig in and defend your ground and keep your feet moving on the offensive and defensive lines. In a stroke of brilliance Bo said that if you give me the ball, I will soar over the top.

Did he ever. The Auburn faithful erupted. Did we just witness that? Did that man jump over not only the Auburn line but then the second level, the Bama line, as well? He landed in the end zone, and handed the ball to the ref. *What?! Crazy!*

It was the first time I had ever seen grown men crying as they left a football stadium. Men with crimson and white jackets had tears streaming down their faces. Men with orange and blue sweaters had tears streaming down their faces. I was so caught up in the emotions of the moment, I felt that I had watched a heavyweight boxing match, and one of the fighters, in a close bout, had snuck in a punch that the other never saw coming. Fight over. (In fact, that was a sentence I used in the article I wrote about the game. Clever, I thought, for a young and mostly untrained writer. I got several comments on it. But I digress.)

The oak trees at Toomer's Corner were rolled with toilet paper, yet again, as they were after every big win. One of the great Auburn traditions was in full operation. Historic Toomer's Drugstore was the public epicenter of Auburn celebrations. This victory over Bama was one of the biggest. The campus was delirious, and we would relish the victory for 365 days.

That's just how it was done in the great state of Alabama.

In my final weeks before graduation, a job fair was held. Even though I was earning my degree in journalism, I tried to keep an open mind and see what else might be available to prospective hires. A college degree was the key into these companies, and if you had studied in a different field, they touted that they could train you to their specific line of work.

The job peddlers were hustling inquirers to come to their tables and job hunters were bustling from one sales pitch to another. I at least stopped by the well-known insurance company, then UPS, the Armed Forces, a major grocery store chain looking for managers, and the City of Birmingham that seemed to be needing several of us to sign up. I mostly just grabbed free pens and chocolate kisses and kept moving.

But on a back aisle of the meeting room, I bumped into the table manned by *The Montgomery Advertiser* newspaper.

"Hi!" the representative energetically said. "Where are you from, and what's your major?"

I had heard this opening line at a few other tables. Must be what company reps are trained to say.

"I'm a journalism major from Sugar Hill, Alabama."

"Sugar Hill! Didn't you guys have some amazing high school football teams? State champions, as I recall?"

"We sure did. Had some incredible players. I wasn't one of them, but I was on the team, going along for the ride."

"We are looking for a few good people to join our team at *The Advertiser*. We particularly have an opening for an entry-level sports writer. You said you were a journalism major. Does sports writing sound like a fit for you?"

What?! Are you kidding me? After circulating table to table, here I stumbled into a job opening in my field of study and interest. Was I dreaming?

"Are you serious?" I blurted out. "When do I start?"

She laughed at that, but noticeably admired my enthusiasm. She instructed me to send in five of my best stories from *The Plainsman,* including, of course, the one on Bo going over the top. Another I chose was a human-interest story about one of Auburn's swimming and diving champions who had lost both her parents when she was 16 in a freak accident. She had pretty much raised herself during her last couple of years of high school and graduated, and went on to become an All-American. Her courage touched many, and she was a joy to write about.

Without a long wait between application and notification, I got hired. I would get paid, real money, to write about sports. I would have a job that reflected my higher education training, right after graduation.

Didn't get much better than that.

14

The One

My vow to not be exclusive with anyone was dealt a fatal karate chop when I met Susan B. Anthony.

Yes, that was her real name. Her parents—Tony, T-o-n-y, and Toni, T-o-n-i Anthony—had loved the story of the early American lady, who had pioneered equal rights for women, notably the right to vote, and had led others against racial and educational inequality. Anyone whose picture was on American currency was definitely legit. Her parents had vowed that if they ever had a daughter, they would name her Susan B.

I vowed when I met her, that if I ever got the chance, I would ask her to marry me.

She was different than the others I had met, fallen for, and wandered from. Betty Jean was an 8th grade infatuation. I often thought of her and wondered what happened to her after her daddy abruptly moved them back to Tuscaloosa at the end of her 9th grade year. Bear had offered a job in the athletic department, and Mr. Asher couldn't say no.

Betty Jean was out of sight, but not out of mind. However, without a relationship with her, or even a continuing acquaintance, it would be hard to justify looking her up in the phone book, driving to Tuscaloosa, finding her and saying, "Hi, Betty Jean! Remember me? I sat across the room from you in 8th grade math class, and we talked one afternoon in your front yard several years ago? You do remember me?! Great! I was wondering, if you aren't too busy..." (oops, wrong line, start over, Joe Billy, deep breaths...); "I was wondering if you would be interested in marrying me?"

About this time, I heard a popular song on the radio by Carol King, called *So Far Away*. One line stood out: "It would be so nice to see your face at my door." Indeed. Betty Jean? Are you listening to the radio?

Just for the record, I was listening. And what I was hearing was clear as day: I can't stop this lovin' feeling.

I had often wrestled with this youthful fantasy. But for sanity's sake, it was time to move on, and try to regain reality. Betty Jean was gone, and it was okay. I would find somebody else.

The others in my smallish circle of love and affection, including Mary Harmon Makowski, Diane from Brundidge, and Rachel from Alex City, had all taken different paths. I had learned from each of those relationships, including that no one of those ladies would be my life partner.

Such is the rhythm of youthful love. It seems to be an almost endless cycle of wondering who's the one, who's not, and what is involved in continuing or stopping the pursuit. It seems that we keep knocking and seeking. Eventually the door might open, maybe just a crack, but open nonetheless. Or it would remain closed. Relationship thwarted. No future there. Knock somewhere else.

I knocked on Susan B. Anthony's door, and it opened. Wide.

I met her my senior year at Auburn in a jazzercise class. I had finished all of my core classes, and requirements for my major except one, and I needed a few more hours in my final quarter of school to graduate. As I plotted out my nearly-completed academic venture, this fun-sounding class seemed a perfect fit. I wasn't totally sure what it was, but it sounded like something I needed to stimulate me physically. I was already glimpsing that the writer's life ahead of me was often sedentary, and maybe I would learn something that would help spur on a life-long habit of fitness. I was all in, complete with the shortish gym shorts of the early 1980s.

This beautiful, lithe, sweaty blond was inescapable from my line-of-sight. She definitely had the moves, and it was not hard to watch her. Unlike me, she showed up at class knowing what to do. She seemed a natural. One of those people that you look at and instinctively say, "How long have you been doing this? I take it that jazzercize is not something new to you?"

One hint that emboldened me was that I noticed her glancing my way a time or two, and smiling. I wondered if she was thinking what Mary Harmon verbalized, that I was 'dreamy.' Probably a little far-fetched at this point, but I could always hope that she thought I looked like someone special, and as such, something would materialize. Attraction might be initiated due to looks, but once she got to know me, maybe she would realize that I was more than a handsome mug from Sugar Hill. (I would have been devastated if I knew that she was smiling because she thought my jazzercize routines were bad, gym shorts too tight and awkward, or my fitness state was trending visually towards 'hopeless'.)

At the end of class one day about the end of the second week, we found ourselves near each other, gulping water. Our eyes met, and it seemed for a moment that we didn't know how to start.

"Hi," I offered boldly.

"Hi." Goodness. Up close and personal, Susan B. was even more beautiful than I had realized.

"You look like a real pro," I offered. "Been doing this for a long time?"

"Actually, I used to teach it, back home at my high school in Montgomery."

"What high school?"

"Sidney Lanier."

"Sidney Lanier! We used to play them in football...eventually got them right where we wanted them...off the schedule!" (It was an old line, and I was trying to be funny. I didn't bother to mention that Jobab had churned up over 350 yards on the ground against them our senior year in a blowout win. I let it go.)

She smiled at my attempted humor.

"I'm Susan B. Anthony," she said, extending her hand after wiping it on her sweat towel.

"Nice name! You don't look at all like you do on a dollar coin!"

"Very funny," she muttered. No doubt she had heard that before.

"I'm Joe Billy Thompson from Sugar Hill, Alabama."

"Sugar Hill?" She asked. "Didn't you have a running back named Jobab Robinson? Seems I remember him running all over the Poets of Sidney Lanier...oh, I get it. You were just trying to be cutesy. You knew that you all beat our you-know-whats."

I admired a woman who knew both about football, and about the greatest running back any of us had ever seen. And also someone who didn't scorn my humor. We might have a connection here.

"Yep, one and the same. Amazing guy. Even more amazing is that he spurned the Crimson Tide and went to the University of the South. He was great at football, but his driving passion was to find a cure for cancer. The kind that killed his grandmother."

Oops. Something morbid and non-romantic had slipped out. Did the mention of death bring in a curtain of pall over our budding conversation?

"I think that's very refreshing. I wish more people could see beyond the heroics of sports and focus on what might be more important."

I wasn't expecting that answer, but I'll take it.

"What are you doing right now? Time for a famous lemonade at Toomer's? That is legal after this fast-paced, heart-pumping, calorie-burning, hyped-up session, true?" I didn't think too much before venturing into the asking mode. I'd better strike while we both appeared to have each other's attention. We might have something here.

"Would love to. Nothing till 2:00. See you there."

First thing I noticed when she walked in was that she had cleaned up nicely. I wasn't surprised.

"Eat here much?" she asked.

"I don't overdo it, but I do like to frequent this landmark. Just has a feel about it that tells me I'm in the right place in the right college town. I live just a few doors down in an old upstairs apartment. So, fair to say I can't resist this place when I get the hankering."

"What's your major, Joe Billy?"

Here was the female conversationalist taking the lead. I liked it.

"Journalism. My daddy commanded that I get a degree in a field I could get a job in. I've already accepted an entry-level sportswriter's job at *The Montgomery Advertiser*, starting as soon as I graduate. I'm pretty pumped about it. What about you?"

Her reply didn't get off the ground, interrupted by the helpful soda jerk. We ordered two lemonades, and with a slight hesitation, I asked him to throw in a hot dog. She made a comment, wondering how that hot dog fit into my post-workout health plan, and I playfully grimaced, and feigned disgrace. I liked this lady.

"I started in pre-med. Bogged down majorly in microbiology, and moved to fashion merchandising. That was quite a switch! But I'm very happy with my decision. Hoping to do an internship with Belk's, based out of Charlotte, and see where it goes from there."

She paused for a sip, and groaned approvingly of the Toomer's classic drink. "Sportswriter?" she seemed intrigued. "Does that mean you covered the great Bo Jackson going over the top to beat the hated Crimson Tide?"

"I was there. If a sportswriter—at least an Auburn one—couldn't productively make a splash and write about *that* game, then pity the poor soul. He'd better choose a different profession. Bo engraved the invitation for him."

And on we went. Hometown reflections of oddities, friends, and family. Stories of ups and downs at Auburn, including classes, sports, and things that surprised us about college life. The more she talked, the more I liked her. And the more I daydreamed.

"I'm kind of tired of Toomer's. Done about enough damage here. Want to come to my place?" I asked. A bold move, surely. I was moving fast, but I felt her moving towards me, and I knew that my intentions were honorable. I felt that if we could shift to my apartment, and out of the public chatter at Toomer's, we would in be a great venue in a relaxed setting for some further preliminary investigation into this budding relationship.

"I'm in."

She never mentioned that she had either totally forgotten about her 2:00 appointment, or that she had decided not to go. The reason didn't matter to me. She was coming to my place.

We talked for hours. I have no recollection actually of how long it was. I do remember ordering out for Domino's Pizza in the middle of it. Someone said that when you are in love, the time you spend together is always too short. I reckoned the flip side was also true: if you aren't meant to be, the time drags and then comes to a merciful halt, doing so when the clock finally runs out.

Susan B. and I discovered that we both loved the Mary Tyler Moore show, and it was on primetime on Saturday night. We started recounting our favorite episodes and vignettes about the newsroom antics of Ted, Lou, Murray and Mary. And on the night went, finding points of connection. I think it was about midnight when she said she had to go.

I walked her back to her dorm and said goodnight. No hugging, no kissing, just electricity. It had been a great day. Anytime you can meet someone for a lemonade in the early afternoon, and keep talking till midnight, throwing in a major change of location, it's fair to say there is something brewing.

When I got back to my apartment, my roommate, Gerald Ferguson had returned from his evening-shift job at the hospital and was up catching a zany, late-night Charlie Chan movie.

"How did it go?" he asked, though not looking at me, but fixated on the TV.

"Gerry, I think I just met the girl I'm going to marry."

"Yeah, right," he scoffed, turning his head slightly to see if I was serious. "I've heard that before." He waved me off, and returned to munching his popcorn, slightly shaking his head at my head-over-heels revelation.

My heart raced when I realized this might be the one for me. In the words of the jazz classic, "I've got it bad, and that ain't good."

After six months of serious and exclusive dating, it was make or break time. We had become intimate with each other, and that intimacy had a deep hold on me. I'm fairly confident that the reader of my memoir will think that "intimacy" equals "physical involvement." It didn't. In fact, our physical interaction was fairly minimal. And while that may seem unnatural, I classified our connection as intimate because we were soul mates. We shared deeply and thoroughly with each other, and showed that we cared for each other. It was an inescapable conclusion that we were reaching a point of no return. Love for each other had taken us to a new location. We were crossing over from a position of independence, to a place of joyful dependence, and it was natural to want to serve one another. We were looking in the same direction, as a French philosopher had mused about a successful marriage, and there was no indication that this shared fixation would ever stop.

In the summer, with my freshly-minted diploma in hand, I decided it was time to make the move. I devised a plan to meet her at her parents' house in Montgomery, ask her father for her hand in marriage, and then present the ring that would seal the deal and bind our hearts. I needed to execute this proposal with precision. What I devised was careful calendar planning.

I was in Montgomery visiting a friend for the weekend and scouting out a place to live for my upcoming job at *The Advertiser*. She was in Charlotte at her internship at Belk's. Best we could all tell, she was loving it, and was receiving encouragement that she was a perfect fit for their company after her upcoming graduation in the fall. I called her parents and learned when she would be arriving back for a weekend visit. It was 4th of July, and she would actually make it a long weekend, as the holiday fell on a Monday. She left a bit early on that Friday afternoon, and by her parent's calculation, she should be arriving around 9 p.m.

I didn't have a fancy speech prepared for her father. I got to the point.

"Mr. Anthony, I have come tonight to ask for your blessing to marry your daughter."

It came out fairly calm. It didn't betray that I was actually scared that he might say no. If he had done so, I had no backup plan.

He smiled, and as if on cue, he dove headfirst into my strategic weakness. Yikes.

"What will you do if I say no?"

"Mr. Anthony (I was careful to address him by name every time I spoke during this somewhat awkward rite of passage), I don't know what I would do, other than wait a while and ask you again! It's quite obvious that I definitely love her—and she assures me that she loves me—but much more than that, I cannot possibly imagine living my life without being joined to her as one flesh. Sir, I assure you, I will honor her, and I will cherish her as a precious treasure until death do us part."

Here I was, venturing into something that resembled vows. My brain was working with my mouth to deliver, on the fly, whatever might sound appropriate. I was at least hopeful that he could discern my humility and sincere desire to become Susan B's husband, with the added bonus of being his son-in-law.

"Yes, Joe Billy, you have my blessing! I am honored that you asked. Her mother and I will support you two in any way that we can." As the reader listens to these words, no doubt there is agreement that there is a certain measured sort of formality in them. Perhaps her father had been expecting it, and had even rehearsed a few times what he would say.

"Mr. Anthony, this is wonderful! Thank you so much! I have an engagement ring to present to her. Do you mind if I come back around 9 to surprise her?"

"That would be fine. First, please stay for an early dinner with us."

I arrived back at 8:45. Mr. Anthony informed me that she had called earlier from Columbus, Georgia. Gauging the time, she should be walking in a few minutes after 9.

"How much have you two talked about marriage?" her mother queried. "I'm asking because I'm wanting to know if you think she will be surprised."

"Quite a lot. We knew early on that we had a special relationship. It just never flamed out. Only grew stronger! So, we started the conversation about our future, and it never stopped. She's expecting me to pop the question at some point. I am fairly confident she has no idea that it is tonight."

Mom smiled. If she had any fears that this could be a one-sided request and desire, those fears had been alleviated. Her daughter was in on it.

Susan B. was late in arriving. I was anxious, especially with the life-changing question rattling in my head. I would not feel any sense of relief until after I had asked, and she had accepted. My plan was to take her into their front sitting room, as it was called, get down on one knee and present the ring, and pray she said yes. Bended knee was a prayer posture, and it fit the occasion. I would beg her to marry me, if necessary.

At 9:45, the phone rang. I assumed it was her. She was obviously late. A flat tire?

I heard Mr. Anthony shout, "Oh, no!" And then he started wailing. Mrs. Anthony grabbed the phone, and I heard her ask for clarification.

As she blanched, I immediately took the phone away from her, and heard the voice of an Alabama State Trooper.

"Mr. Anthony?"

"No, sir, this is Joe Billy Thompson. I'm Mr. Anthony's future son-in-law."

"I regret to inform you that Miss Anthony has been in a car accident, just outside Opelika. She was transported to Baptist Hospital in Montgomery by medical evacuation helicopter. That's all I can tell you."

The rest of the night was a blur. Susan B. had died by the time we had arrived. A Trooper was there to meet us, and we learned that she had been hit by a drunk driver on Interstate 85. He had crossed the median and side-swiped her. As often the case, the alcohol-induced perpetrator had walked away from the scene, basically without a scratch. One other vehicle was involved, but I didn't hear the status of the occupants.

I had never hurt like that. I was, of course, devastated beyond description. But my pain wasn't just focused on me, though I will comment that I felt more sorry for myself than at any time in my life, before or since. I watched Tony and Toni wither and collapse. I wondered if they would ever recover.

If tonight were an indicator for them of any future joy or life-balance, I would guess no.

My world was shattered. The One-For-Me had entered and left. And didn't say goodbye.

Susan B's funeral was held four days after her death in an old, established funeral home in Montgomery. It was packed, flooded by high school, college and childhood friends, all flanking her family who sat at the front of the auditorium. No one had dry eyes. It was obvious to me that we were in too much shock and disbelief to properly celebrate her life, despite some reasonable attempts to do so. Friends told of climbing jungle gyms with her in elementary school; playing dolls and softball, and all the while recounting they knew she was different, a cut above the rest when growing up. Her college friends told how she had comforted them whenever they needed a shoulder to cry on, whether in the aftermath of a boyfriend breakup, a bad exam score, or a change of life-plans. Susan B. had been there for everybody. Her faculty advisor also spoke, telling how she was not just a model student, but she had been identified as one who would do whatever she set her mind to.

It was a low-key affair, very different from the funeral of Old Man Parker. Parker's had been filled with all kinds of singing, and parading, and shouts of Roll Tide. Susan B's was absent the fanfare. Not one utterance of "War Eagle" was heard, nor was there a blue and orange suit in the crowd. It seems that when the old are finally released from their bodies, there is a sense of grief and relief. My observation is that for the young, it's mostly all grief.

I didn't speak at her funeral. All of her friends knew of course that we were exclusive, however no one but her parents knew that on the night she died, I had been planning to pop the question. I kept it to myself. Too painful to even think about at this point.

After the main service, we went outside to the cemetery for another service, a simple interment held under a tent. More tears, more hugs. A menacing roll of thunder in the distance, and immediate thoughts of whether or not we were in for a downpour.

The disbelief kept coming. It felt like news footage you see of high-rising rivers, with the inundation appearing to be imminent. Not sure how's it going to stop, but hopefully it will. Nonetheless, folks aren't exactly sure what to do. Hope is not going to prevent the devastation, any more than the boy's proverbial finger stuck in the dike. Action is needed. But what kind?

I suffered in silence for the most part. My roommate Gerry was there with me. Daddy came down from Sugar Hill. We didn't talk much. Mostly stared at the ground, and shared some bro hugs. We were all wiping tears. Susan B. was a delightful person who lit up everyone she met.

Apart from her loss of life, and all the pain that descended on her family and friends, including me, of course, I found myself wrestling on another level. I had made myself vulnerable to her, and she to me. Now she was gone.

I had previously become vulnerable with several young ladies, and had experienced the agony and ecstasy of not just social dating, but of becoming exclusive, with a move towards permanence. Susan B. was the first one that I had ever met, and with whom I had been exclusive, that I decided that I couldn't live without.

To keep going, I would somehow have to find a way.

I confess that I doubted I would ever again share my heart with another. The pain of brokenness was too great, the wounds too deep. I was certain they would never heal.

I also knew that if being vulnerable meant that this level of pain were possible, I would keep my love to myself. I was certain that I couldn't hack another round of this.

15

The Advertiser

I didn't know how I would keep going after Susan B's death. But I knew I had to, so I found ways to manage my emotions. I had multiple counseling and prayer sessions with my local pastor. I attended a weekly support group. Friends gave me books to read, cassette tapes to listen to. Some days, my grief was much worse than others. There were triggers that caused me to spiral, and each was unpredictable as to its occurrence.

I had determined that one of the best ways to cope was to focus on my new job at *The Montgomery Advertiser*, and stay busy. I had been wallowing in sadness. It was time now to move to acceptance. Hopefully the pain would eventually lessen. I didn't expect it to go away completely, but at least I could reach a place of being able to function with some measure of previous normalcy. I had lost my best friend, and I knew it would take a long while to get back my joy. I was not delusional that the healing would be easy. Over some months, I did notice that my joy surfaced, even if only in short bursts. I didn't fell normal, but I was seeing some movement in that direction.

So, I gave myself completely to my work, and looked for positives.

For example, one of the benefits I discovered of my career was that I would not have to pay my way into sporting events. That may feel like a small thing to my memoir reader, and even out of place in light of the tragedy I had experienced. However, being able to just show up in a work arena I loved, and have a few less practical worries, I counted as a positive. My support group had coached me to look for those, no matter how small or off-beat, and this was one that I noticed.

While there at those events, I could write about what I saw, and put my own spin and deep commentary on the athletic battles of the ages. I would go to the Montgomery Rebels minor league baseball games at old Patterson Field, attend the annual college all-star football game, the Blue-Gray Game, at Crampton Bowl, and be courtside at Huntingdon College and Alabama State basketball games. I would submit my credentials to attend Auburn and Alabama football games, and even occasionally attend practices and press conferences. I was in the big time, and life was good.

I made enough money for a simple apartment near Jackson Hospital, and I ate like a college kid. That was another incentive of the job—the hospitality rooms at most of these events fueled my body with what most would call junk food. I called it survival food. Who was counting calories at age 22 in the mid-1980s? Money was tight, but life was good.

Another thing that helped with costs is that I had a roommate, Mike Dawson, an EMT for a private ambulance service utilized by some of the hospitals. He was usually there when I wasn't, and I was there when he was gone. So, it often felt like I lived by myself at half price. No complaints. However, Mike exited 7 months into the arrangement, and I got left with the entire rent bill. The reason he left is that he got injured coming in early one morning about 4:30 when his shift ended. Seems he ran into a fire extinguisher mounted on the wall of the not-so-well-lit hallway. When he banged into it, it fell off the wall and on to his foot and broke it in three places. After calling his own EMT service to take him to the hospital for treatment, he also got in touch with an injury lawyer I had never heard of named Alexander somebody, whose trademark motto was, "Call me, Alabama!" Alex got Mike $250,000 in damages from the apartment's insurance company (which included among other things, money to soften the blow of 'mental anguish'). So, he moved out, and apparently took off work for a year or two "to recuperate." His pictures from his new residence on the Yucatan peninsula in southern Mexico looked very nice.

As I traveled for work, I started recognizing more seasoned and accomplished writers. Men (and they were all men in those days) from *The Birmingham News* (including a new sportswriter that I deeply admired, Paul Finebaum), *The Mobile Press Register*, *The Huntsville Times*, and *The Dothan Eagle*. Most of them were kind to me, and they at least tolerated my presence. One even told me he had read my story on a star high school athlete from the small town of Smiths Station, and he had complimented my research and persuasive editorial.

The gist of the story was that this kid, with his man-body dominating opponents from baseline to baseline, was tremendous in basketball, but had very little chance to move on to the next level. His small-town background, which had no local newspaper, and his lack of upper classification competition didn't open the door to further play. I said it was wrong. He needed to be noticed. Someone in Georgia read the story (they told me so later) and contacted the kid and signed him to a basketball scholarship for the Dawgs. He ended up making second team All-SEC. Made me feel good.

The *Advertiser* had a few other writers, and particularly when I started, they were all older and more experienced, but my editor liked what I gave him in copy, and he was not afraid to give me some good assignments, assignments you might think were only reserved for more seasoned writers. I was being mentored and encouraged professionally, and that was invaluable. And I had done what Daddy had said: get a degree that will lead to a job. I was loving it.

Daddy had also told me that if you love what you do, you will never work a day in your life. I understood the sentiment of that, though when I dragged back to my apartment late at night, after another round of cold hot dogs and watery soda for dinner at a so-called hospitality room, which I had visited perhaps hours previously, I had no choice but to count that as work.

For the most part, I loved what I did at *The Advertiser*, covering the time from when I left Auburn until I was 39 years old. I guess that means I had never worked a day in my life. I was pressing on, enjoying my life, resigned to the realization that I was a confirmed bachelor who was giving himself to his work passion on a daily basis.

But I would soon answer an ad for new employment.

15

The Reunion

The Sugar Hill class of '79 had a few eager beavers who decided it was time for a 20th class reunion. I didn't particularly feel the need, but it would be good to catch up with folks. I had been gone twenty years from Sugar Hill, four at Auburn and sixteen in Montgomery. It was time to touch base.

I arrived at the Homecoming Party about 20 minutes before it was to officially start. A smiling, enthusiastic crowd was already gathering. Lots of eager handshakes, big smiles, and repeated acclamation were ringing out around the room of "Haven't seen you in ages!" Or, "Wonderful to see you, Mike! You haven't changed a bit!" This cacophony was starting to swell. Partygoers were holding glasses of various kinds of liquids, and trays of finger foods were steadily making the rounds.

Almost immediately I had stumbled into Ralph Jemerson. He owned a fertilizer company in southern Tennessee, and was gushing about how great he was doing. Good for him. Emma Saunders interrupted just as Ralph was starting to divulge last fiscal year's financials. "Aren't you Joe Billy Thompson? I was wondering if I would see you here!" We talked about her marriage, or more accurately, marriages, and heard all about the splash she was making in New York City in the advertising business. She was so excited about her move from Alabama to the capital of the universe, I thought she was going to explode. Then, Sydney Robinson came up, already having enjoyed more than one of the free-flowing beverages, and told of his stellar career in the United States Army, including details of the Bronze Star he had earned for something, somewhere, the details of which came by me in a hurry and I didn't stop him for a clarifying rerun. I listened, nodded, sipped on a Diet Coke, and kept moving through the crowd.

I realized I needed to get properly registered, so I headed across the room to the check-in line. While making small talk with a couple of folks in line, my right facial cheek was decisively grabbed and pinched by an unseen hand moving in across my shoulder. The voice behind this intrusion cackled, "Why, Joe Billy! You are just as gorgeous as you ever were!"

I wheeled around to see the female who was making this loud proclamation and personal space invasion. As I glimpsed her face, I was instantly struck by the numbing realization that I had no idea who she was. Her announcement communicated that she knew me, and of course, in turn, I should know who she was. I'm sure I showed a slight blush, the kind you get when you realize that you are unprepared mentally and caught off guard. We must have been big buddies at one time, right? She treated me like a long-lost dreamboat. It was a small senior class. Surely, I knew everyone?

It took a moment to take in her appearance. I instantaneously deduced that she was a woman who had been worked on. Her hair was a glistening blonde, white mix, presumably helped by chemicals, and cut to a fashionable length off her shoulders. Her skin was smooth and cheekbones high, probably the result of at least a minor lift. Her teeth were noticeably white. Her chest was hard to miss. She pointedly protruded in fine fashion, and near the top was a scrawled name tag that I impulsively glanced at which read 'Mary Jo'. I blinked. The only Mary Jo I remembered in our class was a Mary Jo Hamilton, but she didn't look like this. Mary Jo Hamilton, Class of '79, was quite homely, reserved, almost frowny. There had been nothing outstanding about her physical features. She certainly wasn't the vivacious wonder woman grabbing my cheek, squealing, and moving into position to confront me with her gushing aura.

She got distracted with the next alum coming to the registration table, once again squealing and proclaiming, and I was able to escape. The dilemma of the reunion was firmly upon me, demonstrated in this one example that was surely to be repeated multiple times before the night was over: who are these people?

As the party wore on, news got around that Mary Jo was quite the champion. People couldn't help but talk about her, wondering who she was and trying to imagine how the Mary Jo Hamilton we all knew was this loud, outgoing, formidable female force.

She had married early and moved to Macon, Georgia, where she lived on an extensive and major dairy farm with a regally named Augustus Beauregard (A.B.) Moore, who was some manner of banking tycoon in central Georgia, fifteen years her senior.

I doubt she did the milking.

They had no children. We learned that she was the state tennis champ for ladies over 35. She had hiked the entire Appalachian Trail, and run two triathlons, and hoped to compete one day in the Kona, Hawaii event. Mary Jo and A.B. reportedly owned an island in the Caribbean, but I wasn't sure how that would be verified. And, A.B. gave $1 million per year to the University of Alabama Athletic Department, preferenced for the football program. As A.B. put it, "In case they might need something extra." It's the least he could do, he said, as a graduate of the National Championship Class of 1965.

Presumably because of her husband's extensive focus on his occupational ventures, and with time on her hands, she had earned multiple degrees after attending three different colleges and even became an adjunct faculty member at Bibb County Community College in Macon, teaching fashion merchandising. She was, in a word, something. And that word was spreading.

As the night developed, another tidbit about Mary Jo became evident: she loved to swim in alcoholic beverages. Her consumption of any and all manner of drink didn't seem to slow her down, but she did noticeably laugh more, dance the cha cha with anyone who would join her, and basically command attention. I noticed classmates staring, whispering, openly pointing, trying to discern who in the world was this?

Amazingly, some thought she was an interloper. We all knew about wedding crashers; was Mary Jo a reunion crasher? Had she found a class yearbook, picked out a name either at random (and hope they wouldn't show up), or more probably, work some kind of network to find out who wouldn't be there, and then impersonate them? Or, maybe she really was Mary Jo Hamilton, who had flowered, blossomed, and was now spreading her effusive pollen all over the amazed crowd, casting a spell on all who were in her wake.

She came back to me twice. The first time, she was bubbling, over-joyed with herself. She announced to me in a moderately slurring voice, giggling as she went, "I just went up to Petey Smith. I adored him in the summer of 1977. Had the biggest crush on him, and he knew it. I could hardly sleep at night! Anyway, I got right in his face, and he didn't even know who I was!" My internal response was, "Shocker."

As the party was winding down, she cycled back to me one more time. I had thought I was safe, occupying space on the perimeter of the main room with Monroe Henderson, a football teammate who had played briefly at Auburn before getting dismissed from the team for what was commonly called "personal reasons." Monroe's story of removal had never been publicly known, and I wasn't interested in finding out more. Did it really matter now? As he chattered, he moved his life story timeline to a lamentation about his blown knee cap suffered in his adult basketball league. Not very exciting conversation, but at least I was occupied, and staying sober and safe, and thankful that time was expiring.

Then, without warning, she interrupted. Mary Jo grabbed me by the arm and dragged me away from Monroe a step or two. She got right to the point. She narrowed her eyes, noticeably raised her upper body, flicked the wisp of blondish-out-of-a-bottle hair from her face, lowered her voice, and purred, "What you doing after the party, Joe Billy? I'm dying to hear more about you! I was thinking," choosing her words deliberately in her breathy voice, "we could, you know, go find a place to talk and catch up a bit. You know what I mean?"

Without hesitation, I looked her right in the eyes and replied, "What am I doing after the party? *Something else!*"

At this, she threw back her head, howled with laughter, and shouted across the room, "Hey, Sarah Jane! You won't believe it! I just asked Joe Billy what he's doing after the party. You know what he said? 'Something else!'"

She turned back to me and pinched me for the second time on the cheek while I stood there taking it without flinching. She poured it on thicker.

"Joe Billy, you are not only cute, cute, cute, you are soooo funny! How in the world have you ever escaped getting married?!"

I wasn't even tempted to tell her about Susan B. Anthony. That would not be a fruitful conversational point. I was mostly interested in ending this encounter and getting out of sight from her. So, I simply said, "Just lucky, I guess."

"Just lucky! Well, Joe Billy, you'd better watch yourself, boy. Because I predict that your luck is going to run out, and run out soon! And you are soooo funny!"

Then Mary Jo triumphantly raised her glass to the sky and shouted, "Bartender! I'll have another!"

16

The Musical

The homecoming football game on Friday night was standard fare, complete with homecoming queen and court. Somewhat expected, one of the football players would have to skip the halftime pep talk in the locker room and in full battle pads escort the loveliest lady to midfield for her coronation. The band was in fine form, and expectations were high. I confess it all felt a bit strange, being in the stands and not on the field. Ashamed to admit it, but I had not attended a game since the final one of my senior year. We had thoroughly demolished Hartselle that night long ago. Seems I recall that Paul Washington and Jobab Robinson had even showered and changed clothes at halftime. They wouldn't be needed in the third quarter. They were getting a jump on the hot water supply in the boy's locker room.

In the end, on this Homecoming Friday night, we lost a close one to Ft. Payne, brought about by a bizarre kind of fumble inside the final minute that resulted in what's called a scoop-and-score, a long touchdown run with recovered fumble accompanied by hundreds of gasps, stares of disbelief, and a chorus of "oh no"! Tough loss. Dampened the spirits just a bit, but as the reality settled in, we knew we needed to move on. The weekend wasn't over yet.

That brought us to Saturday night and our class reunion party. Having escaped Mary Jo successfully without any lasting entanglement or embarrassment, I made it to the high school gymnasium for the featured cultural event of the weekend: the Senior Class musical theater production of *South Pacific.* Hard not to smile when I thought about the song, *Some Enchanted Evening.* Mary Jo had certainly been trying to make it an enchanted evening for everyone in her wake. She did have one thing going for her. We wouldn't forget the sight of her across a crowded room. Try as you might, but how could you shake off that lady? I shook just thinking about it. I looked around. I didn't see her. I was safe, for now.

It was open seating for the audience, and I found one near the front. Sat down next to a lady who was about my age. We exchanged "hi-how-are-yous" and I asked her the obvious question: do you have anyone in the show?

"Oh yes!" She gushed. "My Davey is playing Billis, the laundry man! Do you know the show? Billis is really something, a real star! I've been to every rehearsal and can't wait to see how it turns out! Oh my gosh, I'm so nervous!!"

Oh, great. I had gone from the presence of Mary Jo the Magnificent to Musical Theater Stage Mom, hovering like a helicopter over her Davey, who upon discovery by the top talent scouts, was no doubt jumping straight from high school to the Broadhurst Theater in New York City. I smiled and artificially sputtered an assurance that I also couldn't wait to see Davey; I was sure he would be amazing.

I had watched the movie more than once. My mom was a big fan of musicals, and I was pretty well versed in the old-school classics. For some reason, with the overflowing adrenaline in the seat beside me, I found myself just a bit on edge. Inwardly I was thinking, Davey, I hope you don't stumble over your lines during that scene when that parade of nurses dances by on the beach during their morning calisthenics. I'm sure you are something special, but you are probably going to have to prove it. We aren't willing to crown you the second coming of Yul Brenner just yet. Even if your mother already has.

I turned away from Stage Mom to reading the minimal play bill. It was full of short bios, with the requisite personal shout-outs, "Thanks to my family and my friend Tad for encouraging me on! And, Go Bulldogs!" I smiled. They were throwing themselves into this production with all they had, and I was glad for them. The community was behind it, as the ads in the playbill proudly announced wide support. I looked up and saw a few of my reunion classmates in rows nearby and we exchanged nods and pleasantries.

The director appeared on stage to scattered applause, welcoming everyone, reminding them to turn off their cell phones. The cast and crew and orchestra (which was mostly the music teacher playing the piano) had worked for months, and finally the big night was here. They were so honored to be part of the Homecoming Festivities! She thanked the school principal for her support. And, "Welcome to the class of 1979! Y'all all look great! On with the show, this is it!" The lights dimmed (they were obviously supposed to go down all at the same time, but the sequence sputtered, and it was more like a haphazard "Hey, you forgot that button, push that one, too!"). A rocky start.

The opening musical sequence took over from any lighting distraction, stirring us to anticipation, playing bits and pieces of the Rodgers and Hammerstein classic songs, a foretaste of the upcoming production. Then the curtain went up, and we were transported to the residence of a middle-aged French planter on a south Pacific island who was hosting a shapely, cute, American nurse. They were giggling and bantering, like two people in early stages of love and courtship tend to do.

On first acquaintance with the audience, the actor who played the planter, Emile de Beque, was handsome and strapping, with noticeably spray-painted touches of gray hair. He seemed to be ideally suited for the task. Though his French accent wouldn't cause someone to mistake him for a native French speaker who was adapting to English, it was very passable and put me at ease. I recognized that he was one of those high school actors that didn't make me grimace, inwardly hoping for this to be over as soon as possible, even though we had just started. I wondered how Davey's skills would compare to Emile's.

The young lady who was cast as the character of Nellie Forbush, the nurse, also seemed great for the role. I confess that I was probably expecting the worst, that this wouldn't be much of a performance with untrained actors, basic sets and costuming, forgotten lines and blown blocking, and sung lyrics that were probably hard to hear. In events like this I had attended before, invariably at least one of the wireless mics had gone haywire and on the fritz, and that person's lines were lost to all except those in the front row or two of the auditorium. But that wasn't the case here. They were coming in loud and clear.

I glanced over at Stage Mom. She was on the edge of her chair, drinking in the action. She had obviously been to every rehearsal, and knew the show well, perhaps also from the film, as she was mouthing the lines in perfect sequence with both Emile and Nellie. I reasoned that if one of their mics went bad, I could lean over and ask her what was said.

Later in the show, on to the stage burst two children, running, laughing, and playing some kind of game of tag. They were revealed to be Emile's children. What was striking about them is that they weren't white Europeans, like he was, but a mix of European and some kind of dark-skinned race, presumably in the context of the show, some variety of south Pacific islander. Chosen from the local community, the characters were played by mixed-race African Americans, and they seemed perfect.

The sight of the children stunned Nellie. Emile ventured to help her absorb this minor shock. It was clear that Nellie was expecting white children. She would have to get her head around the fact that this man she was falling for had obviously diverted on a path from being attached to someone who looked just like him to having children with someone from a different race. Her surprise did not take Emile by surprise, as you could tell he was bracing himself to explain the background of all this. But I guess you never know how an explanation is going to go until it's time to give it. He tried, but his explanation was complicated.

As the show continued, one of the young American officers, Lieutenant Joe Cable, entered into a relationship with Liat, a young Tonkinese girl, the daughter of Bloody Mary. They wanted more of each other and were taking steps to express their love.

But Joe knew that their relationship, which might give way to a future together, was not standard. He was Caucasian and she was a dark-skinned South Pacific islander. Trouble was on the horizon.

Even though I had seen the film more than once, and should have been well-primed for Joe's reflective song about their budding, messy, inter-cultural love affair, it came at me fresh, like I had never heard it before. I guess I had not paid attention until now. I heard these words:

> You've got to be taught
> To hate and fear,
> You've got to be taught
> From year to year,
> It's got to be drummed
> In your dear little ear
> You've got to be carefully taught.
>
> You've got to be taught to be afraid
> Of people whose eyes are oddly made,
> And people whose skin is a diff'rent shade,
> You've got to be carefully taught.
>
> You've got to be taught before it's too late,
> Before you are six or seven or eight,
> To hate all the people your relatives hate,
> You've got to be carefully taught!

When the song was over, the first thing I remember is that my face was hot, flushing with blood. I abruptly leaned back in my chair, realizing that I had been unaware that I had been leaning forward, no doubt straining to make sure I was hearing every word of the song clearly. I must have had a slack jaw and one of those "you've-got-to-be-kidding-me" open mouths, but I don't remember it. I did notice that my pulse was racing.

Did I just hear what I just heard? Prejudice is taught. It is not something we are necessarily born with, or something that we "can't help," but something we acquire? And we learn it as young children! While not necessarily true for everyone, my spinning mind was analyzing my past, and reviewing my environment of growing up in this community. I mulled over the fact that there really were people around me in my spheres of life who had been taught to *"hate all the people your relatives hate."* Ouch.

I had no choice but to accept the reality that had grabbed my heart. Namely, it was plain to me that my white friends looked down on blacks for reasons that were not acceptable. They had, to put it mildly, been taught that they were a different and superior race of people. The different culture represented by a different skin color on Paul Washington would not be tolerated in a particular swimming pool in Scottsboro. The fears of Jobab Robinson that he would be harassed for any misstep as a black football player at Alabama, were indeed real. They were real because the teaching of prejudice had been very successful, and he knew it. It had been ingrained and passed down to succeeding generations. Those who had been on the receiving end of prejudice knew that it was personal and vindictive.

I thought back to the beginning of the performance. Nellie had revealed to Emile that she was from Arkansas. Emile's language skills stumbled over his rendering of the name of her state capital city of Little Rock, and that drew a laugh from the audience. If one were not careful, that humorous aside could distract the observer from what the writer was conveying. His point surely was that this was not a random geographical placement of the character. She was from Arkansas, in the Deep South, where open and racial prejudice lived. Her grappling with the disconnect of mixed-race children did not just stun her, and obviously upset her, but it would force her to make a decision: was this relationship with a handsome, winsome, wealthy man one that was worth it? Or were her own carefully taught prejudices too much to bear, and she would need to migrate to someone who was "safer" and "more like her"? Nellie and Joe Cable were grappling with parallel dilemmas.

My mind was obviously on overdrive. It's not an over-statement that this artistic representation was a life-changing encounter. Funny how these can happen in the least-expected places.

I reckoned that this perspective of teaching others to hate what you hate covers a whole bunch of things in life. Does prejudice take hold of us, sneak in, and dominate us without us knowing it?

Meanwhile, my mind and heart were now elsewhere for the duration of this senior showcase. I hoped that Stage Mom would not lean over and ask me about Davey's performance. It was an insignificant blur to me, as I had mentally left the building.

But I was sure he was terrific.

17

The *Post*

After sixteen years at *The Advertiser*, I had responded to a random, form-letter ad which was pinned to our newsroom bulletin board: "Sportswriter wanted for the *New York Post*." Okay, so it wasn't *The New York Times*, or *Sports Illustrated*, or *The Sporting News*. The *Post* was known for sensational journalism, cemented as such by their front page headline that grabbed the world: *Headless Man Found in Topless Bar*. If you want to get people's attention, it's hard to argue with that approach. Or, how about, *Why Does God Hate the Mets?* The mostly-hapless baseball team often was the subject of their sportswriters' ire, and their one-liners, in bold print, were memorable. Their journalistic standards were not as high or respected or quoted with the reverence of *The Times*. While they were generally thought of as at least a bit over the top in terms of news and features, their sports section was generally well-respected. Though I had never been there, from what I knew of New York, their overall sensational grade report seemed to fit pretty well.

Maybe my writing would be so insightful, so penetrating, so revealing, I could help change the common perception of the paper! Sure, it was only the *Post*, but it was New York, and that was a far-off, exotic, distant place which I should probably check into some day. The two chances of me getting the job were probably slim and none, but I was

140

thinking I might be ready for a move. If they could just meet me and get to know me, and read a few stories, what was not to love? I was happy covering Bama sports and all, but didn't my world need expanding? I'm sure my ego helped kick in my competitive genes, and I would indeed compete for this job. Sort of like when I entered the Iron Bowl sidelines contest as a kid. Might as well try. One thing is for sure. Nothing ventured, nothing gained.

I sent off a direct and to-the-point letter which told them to please give me a try; they wouldn't be sorry. I attached five of my best articles and a complete resume, and a list of my journalism profs at Auburn who could vouch for me. I hadn't dared to ask my editor for a reference. Wasn't that bold. And then I waited.

Two months later, the phone in my apartment rang fairly late at night. It's the kind of ring you aren't totally sure if you should answer. A solicitor, perhaps, for the Sherrif's Boy's Ranch annual drive? A wrong number? An old friend from high school who was passing through the Montgomery Greyhound bus terminal and needing a couch to sleep on?

"Mr. Thompson?"

"Speaking."

"Howard Usher, *New York Post*." His gravely voice sounded like he'd been smoking for half a century, and one of the big, fat, brown tobacco sticks was no doubt in his mouth that very moment, smoke curling around his eyes and hanging in the low cut ceiling of the newsroom. He coughed deeply, the kind of bronchial cough that you hear and instinctively want to comment on, "You'd better go see a doctor."

"Sorry to call so late. We work late around here. News, news, news! You been reading the news? The President's been in town, the New York Stock Exchange is down, Wall Street is a-flutter, and the United Nations is in session, doing their thing, whatever the heck that is. I've lived here all my life, and have no idea what they do. But they do meet a lot. Anyway, just getting around to some phone interviews with promising candidates for our open sportswriter position. Still interested?"

I caught myself. *Don't appear over-eager!* Of course I'm interested. I'll admit that in the two month lapse, I had sort of forgotten about it, thinking that the long-shot was a dead-end and there was no need to burn brain cells wondering if it would work out. However, I might take the bus tomorrow at 5 p.m. if you offer me the job over the phone. But I didn't tell him that. "Yes, sir. Still interested. I've got a good job here; my editor likes me. The pay's ok, not great (understatement of the day I didn't bother to elaborate on), but I'm making it. Saw your ad, and put out the feeler. Thank you for calling me. I'd love to talk with you." I said all that in my calmest, best professional voice, hoping not to betray my hopes and anxiety.

"Well," (cough, cough), "we need some new blood up here in the Big Apple. You ever been to New York City?"

I hesitated, but portrayed a positive position. "No, sir, I haven't. But of course I've read a lot about it and heard about it from friends who have. Especially the sports teams. Down here in Alabama, one of our state's greatest quarterbacks of all time, Joe Namath, went to the New York Jets. Willie Mays from the Birmingham area of course played for the New York Giants. The New York press called him the

'Say Hey, Kid.' That fit pretty well. Don't forget the New York City ticker tape parade for Olympian track and field gold medal winner Jesse Owens. And, we sent you several famous players with Alabama roots to the Harlem Globetrotters! We may be more closely related than you think!" I was trying both to impress him with a wide range of sports knowledge and stall for a little time as I tried to cover for never having been to The World's Greatest City.

Usher chuckled over the Globetrotters comment. He growled, though not in an unkind way, it just came out as a growl with his chronic voice problem. "Yep, first covered the Globetrotters at Madison Square Garden in 1959. Never got over those guys. When they first came out and that *Sweet Georgia Brown* music started, and they did whatever they do in that passing routine, the crowd was eating out of their hand. Never seen a better basketball team. Darndest thing I ever saw."

I could tell he was pausing to take a few puffs on his cigar. I imagined he couldn't go more than a minute or two without one. He continued.

"I swear. Looked to me like those Globetrotters could beat the New York Knicks with only about 3 players on the court at a time. Anyway, enough of that. I read the five articles you sent. I particularly liked the one about the great Bo Jackson going over the top. Pretty bold move on your part to submit an article from an unpaid college newspaper gig. But I'll hand it to you. You've got a gift. I'm looking for fresh, new blood. Not being familiar with New York is not a liability in my book. I wouldn't mind having someone I can train and bring in on the ground level with a brand new perspective on this city. A man with no debts to society if you know what I mean. Someone who's not interested in furthering his connections. Sometimes up here those connections get a bit shady. I specifically need someone to cover the New York Football Giants. Think you're up to that?"

I missed a breath or two. The New York Giants? Are you kidding? Sure I would miss Auburn and Alabama football, but it was time to move on. A lot of my life was still courtside at the Huntingdon-Samford basketball games. Yankee Stadium sounds like a place I need to be. Quickly.

"Yes, sir, I would love to. If this is a formal offer, I accept."

"It is an offer, Thompson, and I'll see you here in two weeks. You'll start at $38,000 a year. Can only go up from there. You write like you've been doing down in—where is that place, Montgomery? It's like the county seat or state capital or something, isn't it?—you write like that and we are going to know that we've made a great addition to our staff at *The New York Post* (cough, cough)."

Never mind that he knows nothing about Montgomery. Thiry-eight thousand a year? That was significantly higher than what I was making at *The Advertiser*. Woo hoo, I love a raise! It was time to spread my wings and fly north. The athletic competition, the national stage, the exposure for my writing, all of that was of way more value than what I was doing.

A fresh start to life in New York City! Start spreading the news!

18

The Great Atlanta Airport

I had a new job. But having never been to New York, I didn't know what to expect in terms of finding housing. My search for the living space that would be a wonderful new home for me, though, was late in getting off the ground. Literally.

From our part of the country, there is an old joke about the necessity of changing planes in Atlanta. I used to hear at City Barber in Sugar Hill, "Doesn't matter if you are going to heaven or hell, you've got to changes planes in Atlanta!" Those who had flown would obligingly laugh, murmur and nod approvingly. The rest of us, who had never even been on a plane, could only imagine what an unfathomable, busy, and important place was the Atlanta airport. Apparently, all roads led through ATL.

I had flown a couple times, once to Houston to a writer's conference, and another time all the way to San Francisco, when I decided I needed to get out of Bama for a weekend, and *see the world, just for fun!* But that was it. I was basically clueless when it came to most things related to air travel. I figured out the seat belt part, but I wasn't sure about the life jackets, the exit rows, and the gas masks (or whatever those were which dropped from the ceiling, looked real funny with a yellow snout you would wear at a costume party and some flimsy looking elastic straps, and about which I remember being told, "The bag may not inflate, but oxygen is still flowing! Don't worry!" Were they sure of that?) The shake down lines at the metal detectors were unknown entities to me. How did it know the difference in a gun and a belt buckle? I guess it didn't, and that's why most of those places looked like folks getting dressed and undressed in a locker room. A little weird if you ask me.

The day I was scheduled to fly from Montgomery to the Big Apple, via an obligatory change of planes in Atlanta, was a Saturday in September. I had finished with *The Advertiser* the day before. My farewell party, if you could call it that, was a subdued affair. My office mates were too busy to celebrate. The "newspaper bidness" never sleeps. Someone did order in for sharing, in honor of me, some Krispy Kreme donuts and Starbucks coffee, both of which were foreign sights in our newsroom. A few 'bro hugs' and promises to keep in touch, and I was gone. They would mail me my last paycheck. Call back and tell them where to send it.

The flight from Montgomery to Atlanta was right on time. No drama or worries. I had landed in the almost-mythical place called Hartsfield Airport, Atlanta! But when I exited the plane, all heck had broken loose.

We walked into the terminal (which was so big, it looked at first glance like about 50 football fields put together, at least from what I could see), and suddenly we were hearing alarms and being shouted at to evacuate the building. They herded us down stairs, out the building, and on to the tarmac, in the hot September sun, where we waited for news and further instructions. Neither was forthcoming.

Finally, after three hours in the sun, we got the news, along with the all-clear to resume our journeys. Turned out that a crazed college football fan had suddenly realized that he would be late for the kickoff in Knoxville. So, he hurried around people in line and bolted through security and ran to his gate. How he got past those guys with guns and menacing scowls I'll never know. But he did.

I guess in his temporary insanity he figured he would get on the plane, find his seat, and take off before anyone found him. By then it would be too late to bring the plane back. Right?!

He obviously hadn't flown much. Besides needing to know that this breach of security would shut down all flights, he himself would be a hunted man in an enclosed space. It might have looked to me like a space equal to at least 50 football fields, but a deranged Vols fan running through the Altanta airport adorned in bright orange from head to toe would not be hard to find.

They did find him, tackled him (I assume around the ankles from behind, sprawling him out face-first, but it may have been a proper form tackle from the front), handcuffed him, read him his rights, and led him away. I imagined he would end up so far under the jail they would have to feed him with a slingshot. No telling how or when he would get out of purgatory from paying for his football fandom sin.

For the record, he didn't make the UT kickoff against Auburn.

The return to normalcy meant that all of us were going back through the security shake downs. We had no choice. No other way to get to New York at this point. I thought back to my original plan of taking a bus, but how do I get one from Hartsfield? No idea.

What a hassle. We were cranky, sweaty, thirsty and in a foul mood. But at least we could resume our journey. Even if it meant rescreening about 10,000 or so passengers.

The redeeming part of the whole story was at least the unwise culprit wasn't a Tide or Tigers fan, but a Tennessee Volunteer. While our state's fan base was certainly capable of the exact same shenanigans, doing so for the love of team and state, anyone trying that run-through-security-move wearing crimson and white or orange and blue would have embarrassed the entire state. It would have been all over the news!

Thank God for Rocky Top. And for small blessings.

19

The Apartment

For the small-town Southern boy, the shock started and continued. I would describe it as exponential bewilderment.

The crowds were overwhelming, starting with the ones entering and exiting LaGuardia airport after my plane from Atlanta eventually got there. Everywhere I looked, the masses were moving. I thought that the Iron Bowl crowds were jumbled and jostling. They were huge, alright, but those crowds were connected to each other by fan base loyalty, robed and identified by their colors. There was instant affinity. Complete strangers were connected by their football team. That's why people who sat together at games shared high-fives and hugs when something great happened. They were strangers, but they were family. Here, I couldn't tell if anyone was connected to anybody else. My first impression was that everyone was on their own. Though they may not have been, and certainly, the occasional family member shared conversation and affection at the airport, it seemed those were in small numbers. The longer I observed, or moved around to a different vantage point, the crowds of disconnected individuals kept coming. And as far as I could tell, I would always be around people. The taxi from the airport to midtown confirmed this conclusion.

I arrived in New York with two suitcases. Booked a room at the YMCA and figured I would hang out there for a few nights while I got my bearings. I would walk the streets, inquire as to where was a good place to live, make a new home, and move right in. What could be hard about this? Big place. Must have plenty of vacancies.

I ducked into a local diner. When I looked in the menu, the first thing I noticed about New York City prices was their extreme elevation. I had never seen food cost that much, anywhere! Seems like when someone made the menu, they had some kind of fetish for adding zeros. I thought at first the menu was an April Fool's joke. *I'll spread the news alright, that I'm going to go broke in a New York minute.* Why did I think that moving up here was such a good idea?

I settled on a chicken sandwich. Sounded safe. "What do you want to drink?" The waitress asked with an accent that was definitely not Southern. I said "Tea, please." She returned a few minutes later with a chicken sandwich, which wasn't quite what I was expecting. It didn't have that deep-fried, battered look-and-feel, slobbered with mayo and ketchup, or some special sauce, with lettuce and tomato peeking out from the bun, but it was a sandwich. And actually it was pretty good.

The tea, though, was hot tea, tea in a teacup with a bag suspended by a string hanging over the edge, and the whole thing mounted on a saucer. Huh? In Sugar Hill, tea was iced tea, sweet ice tea (unless you needed it without sugar for medical reasons). Hot tea? Was this some kind of a joke? Who drinks hot tea in the middle of the day? And tea in a cup with a chicken sandwich?

I had picked up a copy of *The Post*, my new employer, in the café, and I looked at the want ads, scanning and straining to make sense of locations, configurations, and prices. Yet again, I went into sticker shock. *These apartments cost this much? They must be pretty fancy!* I just wanted something basic. A place to sleep, bathe and eat, and hopefully that configuration would be separate rooms.

I looked in other parts of the sprawling and somehow-connected metropolis, like Hoboken, New Jersey, or somewhere in northern Pennsylvania. But the more I looked and considered, I wanted to live downtown, in Manhattan. I didn't even want to go to Brooklyn or Long Island, but in the most famous section of New York, near Central Park. My brief survey told me that there was nothing in my price range on the Upper West Side, and that was okay. I would probably end up on the northern end, in or near Harlem. I scribbled a few addresses and headed out.

My consternation upon arriving at the addresses was that they didn't look like apartments. Back in Alabama, apartment meant something in an apartment complex, complete with perhaps a sign stuck in the ground near the main office which said things like 'Washer/Dryer Included', or 'Pool', or 'First Month's Rent Free!' But here, I couldn't tell that these were apartments. (And I noted there was not even a place to park your car!) I had seen old-style New York apartments in the movies, but those movies always seemed to be from a previous era, like the one aptly named *The Apartment*, starring Jack Lemmon and Fred MacMurray, or *The Odd Couple*, with the crazy characters Oscar and Felix.

Those were real, old-school New York City apartments. But did they still exist? Come to think of it, I never heard the word 'complex', mentioned in relation to New York City apartments, as in 'apartment complex.' These were just dwellings, endlessly gathered together in buildings that seemed to look the same. Some were obviously of lesser quality, looking almost like what I would call tenements, and some were much better, found on streets with trees and flowers, and they went by the name Brownstones. Some even had guards or doormen. That was the kind of place I wanted. Affording it was another matter. I had little savings, and I had already gotten the message that the salary I had whooped about as being much more than my one in Montgomery was not going to stretch very far.

I even heard the odd phrase that people in New York *owned* their apartment. I didn't understand; how could someone own an apartment, unless they themselves were the landlord? Wasn't an apartment, by definition, living quarters owned by someone else, and you rented from them? It might be short-term, or long-term, but you just rented. Eventually you would move on to another city, or buy your own house, or move in with family somewhere. I didn't understand the terminology. But I started meeting people who owned apartments. How could this be?

I turned from my lustful desire for an historic Brownstone to something more in my budget. I had my eye on one near 88th and Amsterdam. It was in a bustling part of town, both commercial and residential. I was near a subway stop. I would utilize historic Central Park for recreation and fresh air, and I would be front and center to the action of

The Big Apple. Isn't that the best place for a daily writer to live?

But culture shock continued. All apartment owners, this one included, wanted an application fee. Of $500. *Gasp! Are they serious?* What does that even mean? I went head-on with the landlord:

"What's the application fee for, if you don't mind me asking?"

"It's what we do."

He said it so calmly, matter-of-factly, similar to how one would describe what routinely happens in the morning, "Yes, I brushed my teeth." "Sure, I tie my shoes before I leave home." *Of course, Joe Billy! Everyone knows you pay an application fee! It's what you do! Good grief! Were you actually expecting not to?*

"Well, what does it cover?" I probed.

"What do you mean, what does it cover?"

"What am I paying for?"

"Look buddy, you aren't from around here, are you? There are millions of people in this city, and everyone needs to live somewhere. If we didn't have application fees, we would get applications from every Tom, Dick, and Harry, and have no good way of sorting through them to see who was credit worthy. Those who are serious know it's going to take some dough to get into one of these places. That's why we charge it. We are trying to find out who's seriously interested. And besides, it's a lot of work for us. We have to be compensated for our effort."

"But it's not refundable?" I said it with a disbelieving sort of voice, hoping to convey my consternation.

"Of course not! How am I supposed to keep up with who's given me what, and then track down people to give them their money back? They know going in that it's going to cost them. And besides, I've got plenty of applicants willing to pay. Why should I not accept it?"

Never mind that he should probably keep up with it for income tax purposes. But that wasn't my business. Undaunted, I pressed in. "But for the lucky winner of the apartment lottery, you could apply the fee to the first month's rent, or use it as a deposit, or something like that, true?"

He lost patience and waved me off. "Look, this is how it's done. If you want to be considered, you fill out the application, and you hand me five Benjamin Franklins (I don't take checks), and I'll contact you about moving in, if your references pan out."

I was stuck. At 500 bucks a pop, I guess I wouldn't be applying to more than one at a time. I might need to ask if I could extend my time at the Y. However, even that simple accommodation was way more than I would expect to pay back in my home state for a nice hotel. I was steadily learning the hard, economic realities of New York City.

I filled out the application, handed over the money, and went through some kind of beauty pageant process to see if I got chosen.

On notification the next week, I guess I should have jumped for joy that my $500 application fee was not in vain, and then I should have gushingly handed over the first month's rent which was twice the amount of the fee, plus an extra month's rent as a deposit. I found some relief when I heard that in some cases there was something called a 'finder's fee', sort of like what you would pay a broker. At least I escaped without handing that over just to get in the new apartment of my dreams.

I think I mentioned it, start spreading the news: this place feels like a rip-off. I was still mad about the application fee. *Get over it, Joe Billy. That's life in the City. You wanted to move to New York. Now enjoy yourself.*

The apartment met most of my requirements, though it would be tough on my budget. It cost twice as much as the one I had in Montgomery. In this one, the floors tilted. I thought at first my equilibrium was off, but no, it was the floor, built sometime in the previous century. Whenever it was built, the place had the feel and smell of having been occupied for decades. And rarely deep-cleaned.

I soon discovered one problem, and a major one at that. The toilet was finicky. Sometimes it flushed, and all went down the pipes properly. Sometimes it didn't. It just whirled and gurgled and stuck its tongue out at you, daring you to push down the lever one more time. Oh, and you have to remember to never put the toilet paper into the toilet as that is a jam waiting to happen. And you'd better have either a plunger or a bucket handy, because the overflow could get serious. I called the landlord for a fix, but my request was met with either silence, or "we'll get to it, soon as we can", but invariably, the repair guy was late, ineffective, or a no-show.

Two weeks in, I found myself running down to the corner Starbucks to use their facility, though that wasn't easy either. You had to get a code from the cashier to open the door, and unless they knew you or were doing you a favor, they insisted that you buy something before using the restroom. It was, after all, for customers, not for the public in general. It was privately-owned property in a public place. I understood that. But that philosophical awareness didn't help with physical realities.

This apartment was costing me not only extra money on top of my astronomical rent, but a lot of stress, just trying to get some bodily relief. I wondered, "Does life ever get any easier up here in the Big Apple?"

20

The Office

To get to my apartment from anywhere, I passed innumerable people. They were of all shapes and sizes, most were hurrying, invariably running to the nearest subway stop. It was the rare person who was not glued to their cell phone. Blackberry devices had come into use, and people were either staring, texting, or talking.

Oddly, some were just sitting or lying on the sidewalks. They were often wrapped in a dirty blanket or sweater, and positioned on cardboard. They had a MacDonald's cup in front of them, and a cardboard sign asking for money, and the signs always ended with "God Bless." I came to learn that these folks were called homeless.

I had never known a homeless person. When I was a kid we had one for a brief time in Sugar Hill, but his situation was so temporary it didn't compare with the faces I recognized daily in Manhattan. I hadn't known him personally, but Dexter McTavish had returned home to Sugar Hill from Vietnam, battered and bruised and on the wrong track. Someone mentioned he was suffering from PTSD, but I wasn't sure what that was. Every day for a week or so, he would sit on the sidewalk in front of the local Piggly Wiggly supermarket, asking what time it was, asking for money, asking ladies, young and old, for a date. One of his relatives in Gallatin, Tennessee found out about it and came and got him. We heard they took him to the VA hospital up near Nashville somewhere for help, but that was all the information we had. The folks here in New York were long-term street residents, complete with their own culture, system, and coping mechanisms. It didn't appear to me that their relatives would come around any time soon.

I'm sure there were many different reasons as to why these folks were homeless. Some had gotten sick, couldn't work, and couldn't make the sky-high payments required of all who were trying to live and survive in the City. I even caught myself wondering, "Is that going to be me one day? Did the guy who had the previous sportswriter job at *The Post* end up on a sidewalk somewhere, out of money, and out of a job?" I knew this was not a productive line of reasoning as there was no way to know, but it did make me wonder.

Others were no doubt victims of abuse of some kind, spousal abuse, sexual abuse, random violence. They had fallen out of favor with family, and had nowhere to go. Others were mentally ill, and in the midst of that illness were struggling with the compound problems of drug and alcohol abuse. Money was needed to support those habits. Some were just no doubt down on their luck, as the old saying went, and found themselves trying to survive by begging.

I was overwhelmed at the daily sight of them. I even found prejudice rising within as I considered their plight. Were they really in need, or were they hucksters, posers, trying to make us think they were down on their luck, when in reality, they could clean up nicely and actually pull in more money than I could at a decent job.

I was on a subway once, and a man noticed that I had given money to someone who asked for it. In my orientation to New York I saw that some gave money to those who rode the rails and went through the subway cars, one after the other, and asked. Most everyone ignored them. I gave some to a beggar one day. A bystander on the train asked me, with disdain, "Did he thank you?" I said that he had. It was a mumbled thanks, but I had helped him and he responded. The bystander berated me. He said those guys are con artists. They live a life of deceit and trickery and make you think they are in need. Their job is to trick you. He repeatedly scolded me. I listened and absorbed his info, trying to fast-forward as to how I would respond next time when asked. It didn't matter to me that all of their money was tax free, off the record. Mine, I would soon learn, was ridiculously taxed. Howard Usher, the man who hired me, had failed to mention that point.

So, my prejudice towards the homeless was fueled by suspicion. I knew I was not coping with their presence because I had moved away from my original posture of compassion. At first I would stop to ask if they needed anything, listen to their predicament story and occasionally hand over a $20 bill and a pat on the shoulder.

Then, I began ignoring them, failing to make eye contact and just keep on moving. I realized this was my own method of survival. I didn't know their stories, and most likely never would. I wouldn't get to the bottom of why they were in this mess. My prejudice was activated, and I insulated myself from them. In my mental struggle and self-justification with what was right and what was wrong in interacting with them, I figured it was easier to just keep moving. Someone would take care of them and solve their plight. I didn't have the resources to do so. Besides, if I kept passing out greenbacks, I would soon be on the sidewalk with them. That was a bigger concern to me than what they were going to do with the occasional $5 bill I grudgingly handed over.

After taking a week to adjust to my new living arrangements, I found my way to *The Post.* I had ridden the trains for a week, and was getting semi-familiar with the iconic subway system. I was now aware (due to the mishap of getting on a train on the wrong side of the tracks and feeling that I would never get off) that it was easy to go Uptown when you meant to go Downtown. Or jump on a Local, which made stops at all the stations instead of going Express, which went directly to where I was headed. I learned which trains went to the Bronx, and which to the Staten Island Ferry, and which ones eventually led to JFK airport, and also that none went to LaGuardia. The differences in the 1 and 2 trains and the A, C, and D trains, the change of trains at Times Square or Grand Central Station, all were part of the New York living experience. I wouldn't say that in a week I was comfortable, but I wasn't overwhelmed. I at least knew enough to ask semi-intelligent questions of the station clerk, especially when apartment hunting and looking for the best station that was nearest to where I was going. It was all part of my continuing education of life.

At the front desk of *The Post*, I got finger-printed ("Just for our records so we know for sure who you are"), and got my picture security badge for clearance and access to the building. I filled out some paperwork, and then I was escorted into the office of my new boss, Howard Usher.

He looked exactly as I imagined he would.

He was short, overweight with his shirt falling out of a not-so-tightly pulled up pair of pants, unkempt hair, and a cigar permanently attached between his teeth, lit or unlit. On introduction, he coughed and grumbled and complained (about the subways, the weather, the guy selling hot dogs at the corner who didn't give him the right change, but "Heck, I just gave it to him, I'm sure he needs it, but I'll probably go somewhere else next time"), and as he rambled on, he even smiled. I wasn't expecting the smile. Everything in New York seemed so much like bustle, and hurry, and deadlines, and *Why are you talking to me; do I know you?*" My first impression was there didn't seem to be much room or reason for smiling. But I was wrong. Usher, on first appearance was gruff, but the more I sat there with him, I thought he was more like a teddy bear.

Two guys in the newsroom were smiling and making jokes, and excitedly banging out copy on a laptop as they bantered about back and forth. Maybe, I thought, it was a provocative op-ed piece. A young lady was answering the phone with a smile (was it a lunch date she had been hoping for? Or did her $500 apartment application fee just get accepted?). Seeing people smile helped me to relax.

Usher began the orientation. "Glad you made it, Thompson. Good trip up? Find a place to live okay?"

I answered affirmatively without a lot of detail, or a reprisal of Mr. Rocky Top's sprint through ATL. And from what I had experienced with my first few days of New York City life, I didn't want to give the impression that as a

Southerner I knew a lot more about how they should run things around here than they did, so I kept it light and moved on.

"Need something to drink? Can I get you a tea?"

Ah, the old tea trick! The one that comes in a cup, with a bag attached to a string that hangs over the edge into a saucer! No, sir! I wouldn't fall for that one again!

"No, thanks. A glass of water would be nice, though."

Usher pressed a button on his telephone. "Missy, could you bring Thompson here a glass of water? Thanks."

Without a word, but with a faint smile and a glance at me, she deposited the glass and returned to her desk. Young, pretty, easy on the eyes, but didn't appear overly happy to run this errand.

"I swear, we run that girl ragged. Don't know what we would do without her around here. She puts up with a lot in this office full of testosterone, if you know what I mean. I try to protect her much as I can. She's kind of like a daughter to me. You got questions about the City, Thompson, just ask Missy. She can help you."

I nodded. Good info. I have questions, daily, and lots of them. I'll have to feel out Missy to see if she is as willingly helpful as Usher intends her to be.

"Let's get down to business. You got checked in at the front desk, and all cleared and ready to go. True?"

"Yes, checked in and ready. They took my social security number, so I guess that goes with the paycheck system."

Usher didn't acknowledge that comment, but plowed ahead. "Thompson, been waiting on you! I want to see what this Southern boy is going to do with this football crazy, loyal readership that we've got. I figured a writer from Iron Bowl country knows how to handle rivalries. You're just in time! This weekend is THE rivalry game, Jets against the Giants. Kick off at The Meadowlands in Jersey Sunday at 1 p.m. Be a good idea to go to some practices this week and get acquainted. You probably won't get to the head coaches or in to the locker rooms at this stage, but at least you could meet a few assistant coaches, and press corps, key players, maybe even some players that are out of the limelight but great stories, you know what I mean? And be thinking about a prediction of the final score. That's part of the intrigue in your daily columns leading up to the game. (Wait; I would have a daily column? That was news.) Whatever you predict, it will make somebody mad. These are rabid fans, so get ready for it. Coming from Bama, you know about rabid fans, don't you?"

"I'll say. There was this guy in my hometown named Old Man Parker...."

"As I was saying, Thompson," ignoring my anecdote, pulling on his cigar, coughing up spit, and plunging ahead, "you'd better think carefully about that final score prediction. The public will route some calls up here through Missy's telephone that will make her blush. And maybe cry. These folks love their Jets, and they love their Giants. Just ask 'em. They will say things, in so many words in the clean version, 'Who do you think you are to predict the outcome? Are you off your rocker? You got a crystal ball? Don't remember you playing quarterback!' And don't worry; they'll threaten to cancel their subscription to the paper, and all that, but just do what you think is best. Call it like you see it. Write it from your gut, from your heart. You've been around the game, Thompson. You've got intuition (cough, cough). One reason I brought you on is that you don't have any regional rivalry blood, from what I can tell. Am I right? You don't know the Giants, or care if they win?"

"That's true. Down south, we've had the Atlanta Falcons, but they've never excelled. Me and my friends followed them because they were the only team to follow. I remember some loved the old New York Jets because Joe Namath played for them, but that was about as far as pro football loyalty went. New southern NFL teams sprang up, like Tennessee and Carolina, but I'm going to guess the fan base is not what the Jets and Giants enjoy."

"Right again, Thompson. It's a whole different world up here. Just wait till the Jets play the Patriots, or the Giants play the so-called America's Team, the Dallas Cowboys. Talk about hate coming out front and center. I've seen guys looking like they were left for dead in the stands after a game. Admittedly, they probably drank too much and said some things and got what was coming to them, especially since they were wearing the wrong colors, but still, they crossed a line. And these lines are pretty well marked out around here."

Usher's description of pro football mania opened the door to a revelation. As I listened to him, I realized that during the week I had been in New York, I hadn't heard anyone mention a local or regional college football rivalry. There were plenty of college teams in the area surrounding and near to New York City, but where were the rivalries? Where was the Iron Bowl-like intensity?

I made a mental checklist while Usher rambled on about his first days on the job, and how he gave his editor such poor copy, he got sent to night school at NYU for remedial English. His professor there was not too helpful, and so on. I drifted away to thinking about some teams I was familiar with. Would Cornell *versus* Columbia, two New York state Ivys, two members of the Elite Eight, be a rivalry? I had never heard of it. Couldn't recall it being mentioned on *Sports Center*. Or what about Fordham against somebody? Fordham was a downtown NYC university, and I had met someone whose son played backup linebacker, but I knew nothing about a hated rival. Binghamton was a small school; did they even have a football team? (I knew of Binghamton, as it was the alma mater of one of my favorite sportswriters that I would read regularly, Tony Kornheiser, of *The Washington Post*. But I knew nothing about the university.) Syracuse was probably the best football school in the state, and were admittedly upstate New York (which was different from NYC), and had even excelled recently in the 90s, and had often sent numerous players to the NFL, among them perhaps the greatest running back of all time, Jim Brown. But who was their version of an Iron Bowl opponent? And if they had one, was it an in-state rival, or someone just in their conference, like a Clemson or Pittsburgh? I was drawing blanks.

I concluded that there were no college rivalries to speak of in this part of the country. But the pro football rivalries were real. I would have to make the adjustment to covering the play-for-pay boys, rather than the student athletes, with marching bands, NCAA scholarships regulations, and Heisman Trophy talk. These guys talked about being All-Pro, Free Agents, the Injured Reserve List, getting a new long-term contract, and winning the Super

Bowl. My interviewing and writing would need a new focus in a new context. And my paycheck would depend on it.

I didn't understand the basics of New York City food, drink, and apartment living. How would I cover this northern religion, pro football? Why did this new life experience suddenly feel more like a snake pit than a journalism job?

"One other thing, Thompson. And it's a big one. Been thinking about it. We need to give you a new name. Joe Billy—that's your given name?"

"Yes, sir, it is."

"That's not gonna fly up here in New York. Folks find out that's your name and you're from Alabama, and they will be skewering you, calling you Joe Hill-billy, or some such foolishness. Gonna be a distraction. New Yorkers love distractions. Just look at our politics."

He paused for effect, studying my body language. I wanted to impress, and appear that I was in control. I didn't blink. I was actually fine with my given name, though I admit it did sound a little rural and unsophisticated. I didn't need initials like a lawyer, yielding the name no one would ever connect me with, Joe B. Thompson. Or worse, J. Billy Thompson. That was definitely out. Usher had been thinking, and he pressed on.

"What about just 'Joe Thompson'? Ever thought of a name change? Maybe to Joseph William Thompson? Sounds pretty distinguished. When they give you that Pulitzer one day, that name will be a winner! What do you think?"

"I think 'Joe Thompson' is fine. That will be my stage name here in New York. I'm all for a new start."

Usher smiled, extended his hand, deposited his cigar in its usual place between his teeth, and waved me out the door to my cubicle. It was time for Joe Thompson to get to work and learn this crazy city, and especially the high-dollar, bright lights sports mania that it represented. I would be a commentator, and I'd better be good.

When I got to my cubicle, still thinking about Usher's assignment of my new identity, poetic justice and irony washed over me. My stage name was the name of my dad's brother, Uncle Joe, or who was better known as the amazing Uncle Moon Pie. The ultimate Auburn fan. I wondered what he would think about my new *persona*, should he ever find out. How would he feel about his name now assumed by one of his nephews, who was making a splash in an office near Times Square, not far from the annual New Year's Eve Ball Drop. Maybe he would send me a care package of southern treats so that I wouldn't forget where I came from. Then again, Uncle Moon Pie wasn't a care package kind of guy, so that probably wasn't going to happen. But it did provide at least a little humor in what was suddenly feeling like an ultra-pressurized environment, one in which I would have to deliver, regularly and insightfully, for a readership of potential millions. *Gulp.*

I found myself praying. "Lord, help me not to do anything stupid. Some folks say that stupid can't be fixed. So, please keep me from stupid."

21

The Lady by the Window

Locating a place to eat in New York was never a problem. Eating establishments populated Manhattan, with every brand of cuisine from every corner of the earth. The prices and settings varied as well, from fancy sit-downs that required reservations to food trucks. I learned there was a section of restaurants in midtown called Hell's Kitchen, near Broadway, which had to be the worst marketing name I had ever heard of. I am positive that the city council of Sugar Hill, Alabama would never have allowed it, either formally or informally. But here, I guess it was what it was.

I had a favorite place that I liked to slip into on the weekends. There was only one TV, and it was usually overwhelmed by conversations. People didn't go there to watch, but to eat and fellowship. I enjoyed striking up conversations to get the take on the local sports teams, which were usually in a tail spin, or in some kind of diva player or disgruntled coach drama. I didn't bother to tell them that I was a writer for *The Post*. I came across as a local yokel, who just happened to frequent this aptly-named Five Napkin Burger to get my fill of semi-greasy food and drink and be around some other fans. It was a good break from the pressure of the newsroom and the insider-speak of my professional journalism friends. Their food was terrific.

I also had very little social life. I had attended church a few times, but had not really adapted or found one that I felt comfortable in. It wasn't like back home, where folks grew up in a particular church and went Sunday after Sunday. They were not only known to everyone else in the church, and on the membership roll, but they were expected to attend. Here, it was easy to be *incognito*, unaccountable, come if you can, and we understand if you can't. After all, most everyone seems to be working around the clock at jobs and life just to survive. I would keep looking, but as with most things here, it was different. And it would require some extra effort to get settled. I probably needed some kind of small group, or men's group, or something outside of the 11:00 Sunday hour to really get plugged in.

I wasn't a party person, nor a particularly athletic, work-out sort of guy. I did enjoy long walks in Central Park, but my social circle was limited. Life at *The Post* seemed to consume much more time than my previous job at *The Advertiser*. Plus, I was learning a new city, new systems, a new spoken accent, and coping with prices I still couldn't believe. For the first time in my life I was budgeting in earnest. I had heard something about the old "envelope system", popularized by the radio talk show financial adviser named Dave Ramsey: Write a category on an envelope, like food or recreation, put cash in it from your paycheck, and spend only what was in there. When it ran out, wait till the next check to replenish that particular envelope. The system not only worked, but saved me from financial ruin.

I kept one envelope for going out to eat on the weekends. I got tired of the food trucks and the Ramen noodles, and the singular piece of pizza washed down with a can of soda, advertised in a delicatessen window. After a couple of trips to the Five Napkin Burger, it became my place of choice. On Friday nights or Saturdays, or sometimes both, I would trundle off, with envelope in hand.

I had been in New York for about 2 months. It was now late November. I had not even thought of going back to Sugar Hill for Thanksgiving, as the travel was too expensive, and my time too limited. I had opted to stay in the City where I witnessed the Macy's Thanksgiving Day Parade, and it was marvelous! Those floats going down 5th Avenue lifted the spirit. Besides, I couldn't leave; we were in the throes of football season, and the playoffs were looming. Pulitzer Prize-winning copy was waiting to be written—by me—to describe as of yet, unknown gladiator scenarios fought on 100 yard-lined fields. I needed to stay close at hand, attentive, and ready to pontificate at a moment's notice. Usher was at least moderately pleased with my early work, and I wanted to please him. The hate mail I received from irate Jets or Giants fans was actually a good sign. My stuff was being read.

Thanksgiving weekend was the traditional time of the Iron Bowl. My mind wandered back to my student newspaper days at Auburn, when I covered the Greatest Game on Earth. But I knew that chapter of my life had been closed. I had moved on. I had to. I wasn't a New Yorker, but I was a transplant, and doing the best I could to bring some fresh energy of sports reporting for the fans of New York. I even had a regular column. (Usher had told me it would be daily, but it was more like thrice-weekly. That was okay. Easier to stay fresh that way.) I was digging in to my new life, and trying hard to make a difference.

On the TV in the Burger place, the Iron Bowl appeared. I had not actually seen an Auburn or Alabama game since I had left Montgomery. I had a TV in the apartment, and watched as much sports as I could, but time for watching anything besides the New York sports teams was hard to come by. Life was just too full. But I admit I did watch the Iron Bowl with interest. It was fun to observe all the pageantry of college football, which I mentally compared to the somewhat dullness of the pro game which I couldn't help but describe as being a lot about salaries. I enjoyed not being responsible for reporting, analyzing, or filing a story. I could just spectate.

I saw the replays, the further reviews by the referees, the consternation of the coaches, the injured players. I couldn't hear the commentary too well by the talking heads in the TV booth, as the chatter in the restaurant was incessant and loud, but that was okay. I was interested in watching, and not in listening to a description. I sat by myself, and the glorious Iron Bowl kept me entertained. I felt like a kid again!

During a TV timeout early in the second quarter, a beautiful woman caught my eye. She was seated by herself at a table by the window, overlooking 9th Avenue. She did not appear to be overly interested in her food, but was captivated by her cell phone. This, as I mentioned previously in my memoir, was what I often noticed from New Yorkers: cell phone obsession. The world and its knowledge and its interaction was reduced to an amazing electronic tool just a few inches in diameter in size. Connected of course to the outside world by cellular or wifi. *Heaven help us if either of those is unavailable.*

I couldn't help but stare. She was texting furiously with someone, and not showing much emotion in doing so. She wasn't scowling, or smiling, or laughing, but just going about her business. She would sometimes raise her eyes, look to the street, brush hair off her face, and then return to the text toy.

I stared because she was gorgeous. She didn't know I existed, and no one else there did either, so I was safe. I was seated at an angle where she would probably not glance up and catch my eye. I could gaze all I wanted to at one of God's beautiful creations that He had obviously worked overtime on. I don't know if that is theologically-sound thinking, but that thought rolled out freely without even trying or being verified. If I got tired of admiring her from a distance, I could turn my attention back to the TV and the great state of Alabama where the annual edition of the greatest rivalry in college sports was underway. I noticed that hardly anyone else in this New York establishment was watching. But I didn't care.

I found myself staring, but not just because this woman was beautiful. There was something about a mannerism or two of hers, especially when she looked up and brushed her hair with her fingers, that made me think I had seen her before. It was that feeling that if it wasn't her, she must have a twin sister that I knew. I started going through the filing cabinet in my brain trying to discern if I could possibly know this lady. Did she live in my neighborhood? Did I see her on the A Train every morning, and just now, with this long look, I realized I had seen her before? Had I run into her at the grocery store one day a month or two ago, and chatted with her about the weather? Did she work in a neighboring building to *The Post*, and I had seen her enter her office at least once?

It really wasn't a big deal if I had seen her before, just a huge coincidence! In a city of several million, there is a slight mathematical possibility that you will run into someone you know. I had ended up with Missy, from the office, on the Staten Island Ferry one Friday night a few weeks ago. Random, but real. We chatted and were pleasant. There was nothing there, but we were becoming friends, which was hard to cultivate in our office environment. Glad I met her outside, in the City in the midst of its cultural machinations. She's nice. I'm glad to be on the team with her.

As I stared at the woman by the window, my brain fingered a particular mental file and image from my past. It wasn't from my time in New York. Without realizing it, I let go and dropped my onion ring on the floor. This was a eureka moment.

The woman didn't just look familiar.

She was familiar.

22

The Ecstasy

I didn't hesitate. I instinctively got up and went straight to her table. I didn't have to summon courage and think of some lame line, like, "Do I know you from somewhere?" (How would that person know what I know?) I left my plate of food, my ringside seat at the now-forgotten Iron Bowl TV extravaganza, and went to her table and pulled out a chair.

"May I?"

I startled her. I could tell that this surprise move left her without words, but before she could dial 911, I said,

"Betty Jean? Betty Jean Asher?"

Bewilderment filled her face. I knew it was her. She wasn't sure at first who I was, but then it seemed to dawn on her. Her posture started relaxing, as she processed the realization that I was not some random New York City cad or pickup artist or stalker, but someone she knew from Sugar Hill, Alabama, who actually knew her name, and with whom she could connect my face and my voice to her past. That put her at ease. That's not to say she wasn't in a continually stunned state. She was fumbling for words.

When she found her composure, she whispered, "Joe Billy?"

Bingo!

"Yes, it's me! How have you been? Gosh, it's great to see you! What are you doing in New York? How long have you been here?" And so on. My questions gushed out in machine-gun fashion. I overwhelmed the poor lady. But to be honest, I didn't care. I had just discovered, in a city of countless millions, the love of my life from the 8th grade. The only girl I had ever wanted to marry until I realized that this girl had been anathema to me, because she had been Alabama, and I had been Auburn (the reasons of which I couldn't actually remember at the moment. Silly boy. What was I thinking?)

"Joe Billy, you look fantastic! Surprise does not begin to express how I feel in seeing you! I had no idea you were in New York. It is so good to see a familiar face. My goodness!"

Just the way she said, "My goodness!" made me melt. The woman's voice was a knockout. Smooth as polished silver. I would sit at this table as long as she would let me.

She asked me, so I picked up the conversation. I described my life in Montgomery, and the move to NYC, and all the ups and downs of newfound-city life. She interjected that she also had experienced grief over discerning the reality of apartment application fees. Liked to never have found one that suited! Said she spent $5,000 on applications till she found just the right one on the Upper East Side. Oh, well. Nice to know how a few others live.

I volleyed the direction of the talk back to her. Why was she here?

"I moved here last year. My degree from Bama was in accounting, but I hated the work. I wasn't suited for it. I was more of a people person. The company in Birmingham,

Sternes and Raybuck, put me into leadership, but the field was just not interesting to me. They begged me to stay, so that must have meant they liked me, but I needed to move on. I went to Atlanta for a change of scenery. While there I realized that I liked to listen to people and their problems. I like to think I'm good at helping them through tough spots. So, I became a therapist. It's a long and winding road of education and interminable practical experience to get to the point of actually being able to do it on my own, but I'm glad I did.

"I've had tons of work here in New York. I never even heard of a therapist in Sugar Hill, wouldn't have known what one was. Rarely did I come across one in Atlanta. But in New York, they are plentiful and needed. I admit I have found deep satisfaction in being there for people. However, I got into a rut. I felt like I was hearing the same story, but from different people, day after day. Overachievers in business, finance, law, government, politics, sports, the arts. Most of them millionaires, or better. Never had a problem getting paid! And paid handsomely I might add. But I found myself wanting to do something just a little bit different. So, I answered an online ad for a counselor-therapist in a ministry to the homeless here in New York. I've been working with them since the spring of last year. I have found my place."

She paused, and sipped her tea out of her cup. I tried not to appear to be obvious, but I about gagged. I hid my shock with a muffled cough. If I had been drinking the dreadful hot tea stuff, I'm sure I would have spewed it all over the plate glass window. Working with the homeless? Really? These guys sprawled out all over the sidewalks?

Guys that I can't figure out, and that I avoid because they just look like they should be avoided? Ministry to them; how is that working out?

"Joe Billy, this is what I was born for. They are people just like you and me. They are like folks back in Sugar Hill. In fact, a couple of folks I've talked to recently are from rural Alabama. They came here seeking their fortune and a new life, and ended up on what we used to call skid row. They've had some bad breaks. Many of those bad breaks they've brought on themselves through bad decisions. Often, they have not been willing to take responsibility for those wrong choices. But I'm helping them to face reality. I'm helping them to see that change is mandatory, and it's also mandatory that it start with them. We dig down through their circumstances and mental illness and coping mechanisms and find the first steps to take towards healing."

I was staring into the most beautiful blue eyes I had ever seen, trying to absorb what I was hearing. There was much more to hear about her work, or ministry, she called it. I had a lot to learn about the homeless, and this lady would be my teacher. Maybe I would hurdle over my prejudice. If anyone could help me, I guessed she would be the one. But before going there, I had to ask:

"Are you married?"

"No, never have been. Met a doctor at Emory Hospital in Atlanta and fell hard for him. Gracious, he was good looking. Didn't know my heart could beat that fast. A real head-turner, that guy. Smart and rich. The complete package, right?! Thought we were going to get engaged. We talked about it multiple times. Turns out he was more into himself than me. Maybe my therapist training was good not just for others, but I used it on myself! I recognized patterns in him that bothered me to no end. I confronted him with his own profile, and he turned tail and ran. The thought of being analyzed by a shrink sleeping in the same bed with him must have unnerved him. I understand he married an ER nurse and had some babies and is no doubt living happily ever after. I don't miss him."

She didn't say it wistfully, or in that sort of way in which you try to talk yourself into believing something you shouldn't. She sounded certain, mature, her head on solid. I was desperately attracted.

"What about you, Joe Billy? Married?"

"No! Tragic story actually. I dated several girls, and got interested more than once. My senior year at Auburn, I finally found the right one, *the one* I couldn't live without! But on the night I planned to propose, she was killed in a car accident."

"Oh, Joe Billy, I'm so sorry!"

"Thank you. It's been a tough road, but I have moved on. Had no choice. Since then, I just haven't entered into another serious relationship. Haven't found the right one. Still living the single life. Actually, I've been working so much, I just haven't put effort into meeting anyone. Takes a lot energy to do it right! But maybe one day. I'm definitely open to it. Just haven't gotten there yet."

If she only knew I wanted to propose tonight before she left the building. I actually had rediscovered another special someone that I could live with forever, but she didn't know that yet.

She fumbled for her cell phone. I realized she had not glanced at it the entire time we had talked! *I knew it, I knew it. I had captivated her! Who knows where this might lead.* In my presence she had forgotten the ever-present Blackberry device in the palm of her hand. But now she was back to reality, staring at the screen.

"I've got an appointment, Joe Billy, I need to go. The director of the housing shelter has someone lined up for me to talk to. I understand it's a single mom with three small children. They've been sleeping in High Bridge Park, and there are some serious issues in play."

"Sure, I understand." But I didn't let her get out of my sight without a fight.

"Betty Jean, what about tomorrow? Can I meet you here at about the same time? The burgers are great, and I hope you will find the company from your previous small town in Alabama to be even greater." I hoped at the least my disarming smile would cause her to respond positively, especially if she might be leaning towards saying no.

"Absolutely. We've got a lot to catch up on."

23

The Return to the Napkins

I got there early. Couldn't remember exactly what time I had arrived the day before, but I didn't want to be late. I would hang around till she arrived. I had no other schedule.

Alabama had beaten Auburn the day before, and beaten them pretty handily. I was a bit surprised, as I thought Auburn had a better team than that. I could just imagine the debates and arm chair Monday afternoon quarterbacking going on at City Barber. Many of the old fellows had passed on, but there were still enough there to keep things heated and lively. I felt a twinge. I would love to be in the midst of those guys again. Their logic and argumentation were priceless.

What would I say when Betty Jean showed up? Something juvenile like, "How's your apartment?" Or, "This New York weather is crazy!" Or how about, "I can't believe how much a taxi costs from my place up to West 139th!" My day dreaming and mental script-writing stopped when she walked in. Betty Jean was stunning. The most natural beauty of anyone I'd ever seen. I couldn't detect one ounce of her putting on airs. She was the real deal. How was this lady still unattached? I told myself not to try to figure it out. Just enjoy.

I didn't need any of the possible conversational lead-ins. She began with, "Have you seen anyone else from our class recently?"

That was an easy one. "No one but you. Haven't been back home in a while. What about yourself?

"Remember Jobab Robinson, the football player? I ran into him at LaGuardia airport not long ago."

"Remember him? The greatest football player I ever saw. No offense to Paul Washington, but this guy was just a step ahead. Where did he end up?"

"He's been at the Mayo Clinic and the Cleveland Clinic, and has been working on several different specialty medical teams. I snooped online and found out that he's making quite a splash in his field. He's still determined to find a cure for cancer. Nothing stops that guy. I always admired him."

"Brilliance is worth admiring. He was in a league of his own. What did he say about his studies and his family life? I've lost touch with him, and have no idea if he got married, or what happened."

"There was some personal drama before he left the University of the South. With his exceptional brain, he graduated in two and a half years. The football coach got mad when he realized that Jobab was leaving Suwanee for a graduate studies Rhodes scholarship at Oxford to delve into the latest cancer research with the Medical Society of Great Britain. Coach even went to the faculty to protest, saying there's no way J's college education could be complete in that time frame. They showed coach the transcripts, and apparently after seeing them, he walked out of the admin building without saying a word. J had set 12 school rushing records, doing so in only two full seasons. Besides that, he had obliterated every track and field record in sprints. After finishing his Master's degree at Oxford, he got married and had a baby. Turns out he had a son and gave him a Bible name, from the book of Chronicles, just like his. You ready? He named him Happizzez. Wanted his son to have a name that he did not hear of in any other family. I think he won the prize with that one! He said it sounded, well, you know, happy!"

We shared a laugh on that one. This was indeed the first Happizzez I had ever heard of.

"How did it go with the lady you went to talk to?" She had started with a blast from the past in bringing up Jobab and his whereabouts. I figured I should build on the shared experience of our exit conversation yesterday.

I found it easy to talk to Betty Jean, unlike when I was admiring her mostly from a distance in junior high, petrified that she might actually say something to me and I would sit there like a house by the side of the road, not finding any air in my voice to respond.

"The lady was so sweet. I met her children, and they are precious. She's a victim of abuse and abandonment. This lady had lived in a beautiful suburb in Cleveland, Ohio. Came to New York, following her husband and his fancy new job in the heart of Wall Street. Two weeks here and he put her in her place, smacking her around and running her out of their house and apparently going after multiple women. Terrible story. It's like he lost his mind or something. We are helping her to find a safe place, get her daily needs met, get counseling, and try to get back on her feet. As for most of the people I talk with and listen to, it's a long road to healing. But it's got to start somewhere."

I admired this lady. She was making a difference in people's lives, daily. That was obvious. I didn't know anyone else doing this kind of work. I could only imagine, though, that she made everybody feel good who was privileged to have time with her. Just looking at her made me feel good.

"Okay," I said, trying to deflect from the homeless just a bit, "tell me about the most interesting counseling session you've ever had."

I had ordered two chocolate shakes and two burgers. I loved a woman who wasn't counting calories. While waiting for the delivery, she pondered just a moment, and then dove in.

"I was interning in Atlanta. A lady came to see me who said she had a serious problem. She was obviously hiding something, struggling to know how to broach the subject. There were long periods of silence. I tried to draw it out of her, and finally did through the question, 'What's the main thing this is about?' She said it was about a secret she had been keeping from her husband of 25+ years.

"That sounded serious. Not that I hadn't encountered such a problem before, even in my somewhat limited experience up to that time. Secrets are often the subjects of counseling sessions."

She momentarily paused as the burgers arrived, steaming and oozing deliciousness. I started in, feeling sorry for her that she had the floor and couldn't eat and talk at the same time. I quickly put aside my personal shame and guilt. This place was burger heaven. She continued.

"The lady said she had never told her husband that she was an Auburn fan. He was Bama through and through. She had pretended to be Roll Tide, and all that. Said his head would explode if he had any knowledge that she was from the dark side. She played the part perfectly of the faithful Bama wife with the maniac Bama husband, even going on road trips to Starkville and Gainesville and Baton Rouge, and who knows where else, but it was all an act."

The very mischief! This was a great story. She took a bite of burger, groaned approvingly, used just one napkin to wipe the residue, and went on.

"The worst part was, she said, was that she had not only been an Auburn fan, but before she had met her husband, she had been engaged to a former Auburn football player. She had never revealed it, and it was eating her alive.

"I asked her, 'So, what's the problem? You've been happily married, right? It's only a football loyalty', or at least I tried to frame it that way.

"She said she had been happily married, and they had three children who were Bama fans. And I noted she didn't say, those three kids were happy and healthy, or wealthy and accomplished, or successful and beautiful. They were first identified by their mother as Bama fans.

"But she said this whole thing felt like adultery. She had not been totally honest with him in the area of life that was the most important to him, and that was Bama football. It wasn't a 'house divided' as the common saying goes in Alabama, where one spouse is for Auburn and the other for Bama. Those are openly divided situations. They don't hide it. This one was a secretly divided house. This was worse.

And the situation was imploding. She was heading to a nervous breakdown unless she got a breakthrough."

"What did you do?" I asked before distracting myself with a slurp from the chocolate shake. The whole thing was humorous to me, but I tried not to laugh. Putting my mouth to work with food rather than using it as an outlet for an emotional response I might regret later was a good move. Really? Marriage problems over a secret, unrevealed love affair with an Auburn Tiger? I was dying to know how the trained therapist Betty Jean Asher directed traffic on this latest version of the end of Western civilization as we know it.

"I looked her right in the eye, and said 'War Eagle!' She was stunned. I don't know what she was expecting, but that wasn't it. I told her to tell her husband to 'man up' because she had some hard news for him. It was obviously crushing her, and she needed to come clean. It should be a tribute and honor to him that she turned her allegiance over to Bama, even after a lifelong affinity with the Orange and Blue. If he couldn't take that news, then he was a wimp."

"What happened?" I asked.

"Craziest thing. When she gave him the news, he clammed up and didn't say anything for like three minutes. Finally, with his eyes wet with the initial stages of tears he admitted that before they got married, he had been engaged to an Auburn cheerleader. He had never had the heart or the gumption to tell her. They both ended up laughing hysterically, and the whole thing blew over, and the next thing I knew, they went to southern Mexico on a second honeymoon. *And they did it on the third Saturday in October, the sacred day on the calendar of the annual Bama Tennessee game.*

Imagine a hard-core Bama fan doing that! Their souvenir from that trip was another baby on the way. End of the story? They named that baby, *Aubie*. What a hoot!"

We kept trading stories and laughter and the time flew by. I didn't know it was possible for this establishment to close in the City that Never Sleeps, but we stayed at Five Napkin Burger until they announced they were actually closing and going home, to sleep. I told the maître d' that we were old friends just catching up after many years apart, and their restaurant had provided a perfect setting for a twosome reunion. Uncharacteristic of a broke sportswriter, I slipped the man in charge a $20 bill for the extra space we had taken up, and the extra attention we had gotten during what must have felt in football years like seven overtimes. We just couldn't quit.

We went outside. The nighttime November wind was blowing and I wrapped her in her sweater. She almost cooed approvingly. I was smitten. I touched her hand, without regret, shame, or apology, but I dared not get any closer. By now, I was sure she knew I was totally obsessed with her, and yet I didn't want to blow this chance. I would rein in my emotions and take a mature, patient approach. If it was right—and I believe God had directed our steps to the same burger joint on the same day—she would still be available and interested tomorrow. If not, then it wasn't meant to be. Perhaps that was a fatalistic sort of approach, but I didn't care. I had loved this lady longer than she knew it, and I was closer than I had ever been.

Surprisingly, she made the next move.

"What are you doing next Saturday afternoon, Joe Billy?"

I wanted to blurt out, "Whatever you're doing," but I played it more coy than that. "Nothing I know of. Getting ready for the Giants-Rams game on Sunday with some last-minute preparation, but they are at home, so I'm not flying anywhere, but off that day. What do you have in mind?"

I was wondering if she was going to ask me over to her place, or take a long bike ride through Central Park, or she had two tickets to a Broadway show and was I interested. She surprised with her answer:

"Miss Truby's Bar and Grill near here on West 47th Street hosts Bama games on TV on Saturdays in the Fall. You'll be surprised at how many Bama fans live in New York. Plenty of them come to the watch party! It's sort of like a tailgate event, but it's inside and with mostly people you don't know. Next Saturday is the SEC championship game. Bama is in, and will play Florida. Meet me there? Kickoff is at 4. Think an Auburn boy can handle it?"

Forget Auburn. I was a Betty Jean fan. I would be there.

24

The Tailgate Party

The next Saturday morning I finished my prep for the Giants-Rams game. I was enjoying my work much more than I had in Montgomery. It was due to some kind of combination of work plus daily living that was giving me an extra spark. There was something about this place that was captivating. I had started to notice that people who lived in New York City liked it. That struck me as odd, because this place has tons of drama, inter-cultural miscues and potential mishaps, and I haven't even gotten to the extraordinary financial bits, which I think I've mentioned a time or two. I couldn't recall meeting anyone yet who felt trapped and wished they were somewhere else. New York was special.

Today I would cross another bridge in my orientation to The World's Greatest City. I would discover the Alabama football fans who lived in the five boroughs of New York. I had been counting the days until I activated Betty Jean's invitation to join her at Miss Truby's Bar and Grill on West 47th Street.

Again, I thought it a good idea to be early, so just after lunch I started making plans for departure from my apartment. I wanted her to know that I was punctual and eager, and that this was the only thing on my schedule. Despite the crowds and TVs and adrenaline that goes with great college football, Betty Jean would have my full attention.

As I opened my closet, which in my sized apartment was more like a place to hide things instead of hang them properly, I was struck by a wave of attire distress. What would I wear?

I couldn't show up in Auburn garb, of which I had several choices. If there were true Alabama fans there, and I assumed they would be, that would elicit all kinds of distracting comments. I wasn't interested in defending the Auburn running game or special teams or imminent coaching change. That might get me off my game, which was to impress Betty Jean with my presence. She, of Crimson Tide loyalty, would certainly notice. I didn't think she would mind hanging around with an Auburn guy, and she had even acknowledged my loyalty when she gave me the invitation. But I was wanting to support her, and dressing appropriately seemed like being one step closer to her heart.

My life journey from rural Alabama to New York City had caused me to take a deep, personal inventory. I was a proud graduate of Auburn University. I was a partaker of the traditions, the legacy, and the heritage of that great school. I was an Auburn fan, no denying it! Though not as boisterous and over-the-top as Uncle Moon Pie, I was a lifelong supporter of the Auburn Tigers. There wasn't any doubt wherein my loyalties lay.

However, I encountered some serious questions that had never surfaced until this afternoon: did my Auburn affinity mean that I could never cheer for the Crimson Tide? Would doing so be considered "fandom blasphemy"? Would

I be ridiculed and scorned, and called a turncoat by those for whom team loyalty was one of the highest values in life? More basic than that, could I support in any way the number one rivalry opponent of Auburn University, or would my lot in life be that of a strict antagonist to any Bama success?

In my ongoing, quiet reflections on my new life outside the great state of Alabama, I found myself drawn back to the place. Not attracted enough to leave my job at *The Post* and return home, but I felt some pride for my home state that I didn't summon from within when I lived there. It's almost as if I had to leave before I could see what I had. I was proud of my home state, of my friends. The place immortalized in the song *Sweet Home Alabama*, and whose state motto was 'Alabama the Beautiful.' Sure, I was a graduate of Auburn, but did that mean I could never cheer for the Tide? Did I really have to choose one over another, and thus love one and hate the other? Or, could I embrace both Auburn and Alabama as having consistently great football teams, not to mention being excellent places of higher learning.

And why did loyalties have to be reduced to either one of those two? What about University of South Alabama, or North Alabama, or West Alabama? What about Troy, for Pete's sake? They had a great football team, even though they were always left out of the conversation. What about Montevallo, or Samford, or Birmingham-Southern? Could I not respond with pride to any mention of any university in the state of Alabama, and openly say, "Yes, they are part of what makes our state so great!" I am partial to Auburn, for a number of reasons, but I'm happy for the success of any of our schools. Easy enough to say that for Montevallo, perhaps, but was I ready to extend those kudos of success even to the perennial football power based in Tuscaloosa?

I had never heard anyone try to do that, but I was talking myself into it. I would wear something today that I had never considered in my life. It didn't matter that I had worn orange and blue for as long as I could remember, dating back to my favorite footy pajamas when I was 3 or 4 years old.

A reader in Dothan had heard that I had moved to New York. He said he had admired some of my columns in *The Advertiser*, and thought he would send a 'relocation gift', hoping I wouldn't forget my roots. The content of this package from a random fan reader was a white Bama jacket with the emblazoned Crimson script *A* on the pocket.

I had never worn it. Using the 'b' word again, it would be considered blasphemy to show up in public, for me, as an Auburn man, to wear the colors of the enemy. If someone saw me who knew me, they might never speak to me again. Or at least would address my mental health issues, if not on the spot, by getting the rumor mill started on the telephone circuit. *"Did you hear about Joe Billy? No, well, let me tell you."*

I fingered the *A*. I thought of the great teams represented by it, and all the gridiron success they had. They had made their fan base proud. Bama had been a national champion many times over, and had brought fame and some fortune to the state because of it. There were only a few other places that shared that kind of success. The list was short. Schools like Michigan, Notre Dame, Oklahoma, Ohio State, USC. Wherever I went in New York and people discovered I was from Alabama, they wanted to talk football.

I admitted the football talk that came out was about Bama and not Auburn. Was that so bad? At least it was an entry way into other points of conversation about our state.

This *A* was the one that Old Man Parker had lived for, and eventually died because of. Uncle Moon Pie despised it with every ounce of his being. The *A* represented the enemy, and he would not under any circumstances, fraternize with or provide aid to the Enemy. But I couldn't hold that against him. It was the life that he knew. He couldn't escape it.

What was Alabama known for besides football? This *A* turned people's mind not just to a school but to a state. It was a state that had plenty of recent history coming to the fore. Admittedly, some of it wasn't so pretty.

Again, I will mention George C. Wallace standing in the doorway at the University of Alabama. He later said that his words were only reflective of what Alabamians had wanted him to say. His missed on that one badly. The little demagogue didn't wear racism well. His prejudice did not allow him to think or see clearly. And by the way, those students got in, with federal intervention.

Alabama was known for the Civil Rights Movement. Selma. Rosa Parks. MLK.

And yes, Forrest Gump.

Gulf Shores was beautiful, and attracted vacationers from across the land. And there was Marshall Space Flight Center in Huntsville, and Birmingham, the steel capital of the South. But it always seemed to cycle back to the fact that Bama was known for great football teams. And the University of Alabama was one of the best. This jacket was emblematic of their success.

Though I could hardly believe I was doing it, I took the jacket off its hangar and put it on, slowly, carefully, almost frightfully, like when you do something you've never done before and you could swear it's wrong, but you've already decided to do it so you might as well go through with it. Time to experience it.

I stared into the mirror. *Was that really me?* I ran my finger over the outline of the Crimson *A*. I couldn't help but make the connection: it felt like another famous A in history, a Scarlet one.

In some odd sense, this also felt like adultery.

I zipped it up, and headed out to meet my mistress.

Miss Truby's was hopping when I got there. Ten big screen TVs were blaring, all tuned to the same Bama pre-game show. Wait staff was bustling with drinks and hot wings and setting up tables with miniature crimson-background Bama flags. Kickoff was still an hour away and the crowd was growing. I felt my pulse racing just a bit at the building excitement.

No sign yet of Betty Jean. But that was okay. I would have a few minutes to work the crowd. Get to know my audience.

I met Richard from Mobile. He had moved to New York to attend Columbia University. He was thrilled that there was a college-football based community he could relate to! Had been to many Bama games, and tailgate parties, and this was the next-best-thing to being there. He had a girlfriend with him who looked a lot less interested. She must have been pulled into his world to see how it was done. Christmas shopping season had just started, and maybe she had wanted to go to Macy's instead. But didn't a championship game take priority?

Sharon from Leeds, just outside of Birmingham, was even more excited than Richard. She greeted me with *Roll Tide!* No doubt inspired by the sight of my jacket. I mumbled (or was it 'muffled'?) the foreign words, "Roll Tide", in return, but they were forced. I could hardly believe I just said that.

She certainly looked the part. Crimson and White from head to toe, complete with crimson shoes, Script *A* earrings, and a wedding band that was undeniably Bama-influenced. She had somehow convinced her husband that crimson and white were beautiful colors, instead of the old stuffy gold or silver. Weren't those so, you know, ordinary? Everybody's got those! She was a sight.

Then it happened, the first bear hug of the day. And that from someone I didn't know. I didn't realize it would be the first of many. Strangers hugging strangers.

Cal from Montgomery was a very large black man. Said he had played for Bear back in the late 70s, but he didn't elaborate. He obviously spied my Crimson *A* jacket and grabbed me like I was his prodigal brother just returning to the good graces of the family. Getting that close to him, I recognized that he smelled a little bit like one of the brewing companies, but he wasn't over the top, at least not yet.

"Are you pumped?" he shouted.

"Oh yes!" I replied. "Can't wait for that kickoff. Gonna make some meatballs of those Gators today!"

He thought that was the funniest thing he ever heard. Slapped me on the back and I thought my vertebrae would disconnect. Note to self: don't sit near Cal.

While I turned away and started rubbing my lower neck area, an announcement blared over the establishment's intercom system.

"Hey, everyone, Roll Tide, and may I have your attention, please! We are so glad you are all here, and more are coming in to join, which is great. I want to remind you fine people of two things. One is that your dues for this year as part of the NYC A Club are due. The proceeds go to provide a scholarship for a lucky student from New York who wants to migrate south to God's Country and go to the best university in the USA. And secondly, a silent auction is being held on valuable items found on the left-side of the bar. Money raised there also goes for the scholarship. And did I mention, *Roll Tide Roll!*"

The hubbub quickly resumed, while a lady walked straight to me without darting her glance. She was intense and determined. Stuck out her hand.

"Lindy Lou, from Auburn. And you are?"

"Joe Thompson. Formerly of a small place you've never heard of, Sugar Hill, Alabama."

"Don't be so fast, Bama boy. I've heard of it! Didn't you have a running back in the late 70s named Jobab Robinson?"

I was impressed with that comeback. Was she a sportswriter?

"Sure did! How did you know him?"

"I saw him play in the state All-Star game his senior year. Something about small town Sugar Hill sticks in my mind as being his hometown. He was sort of unforgettable. On his way to the end zone, *again*, Jobab rolled over my big, bad, high school nose guard of a boyfriend who thought he was ready to jump straight to the NFL. Jobab flattened him out on Legion Field and left him for dead. Boyfriend never played another down. Skipped college, went into real estate and now works for some guy I've never heard of whose face is plastered over billboards from east to west advertising some kind of legal services. Alexander somebody. Enough of that! Can't believe neither Bama nor Auburn landed Jobab. Went somewhere, I don't even know where."

"University of the South, Sewanee, Tennessee."

"Where?"

"University of the South. He was more interested in school than sports. He loved their biology department."

She looked at me like I was speaking Russian. Obviously, this was not computing.

She regained her composure, and said, "He was amazing. You knew him?"

"Oh, yeah. I played on the same team with him. Watched him run away from every would-be tackler in the state of Alabama. But with world-class sprinter speed, he was not to be caught. J and I go back a long way. Exceptional person."

"What's he doing now?"

"Still trying to cure cancer."

Lindy Lou thought that was hilarious. When she calmed down, she realized I wasn't joking. The conversation changed to today's event. I made the next move.

"Say you're from Auburn? What are you doing at a Bama party, if you don't mind me asking."

"I love me some Crimson Tide. I may be from Auburn, Alabama, but don't let that fool you. Daddy opened a trucking business there, connecting shipping of goods from Montgomery to Atlanta and beyond. But he was born in Tuscaloosa and was Bama through and through. I caught heck from my friends growing up. They never could get their heads around the fact that a girl living in Auburn didn't worship at Toomer's Corner. But I survived. And you?"

"I moved up here a few months ago. I'm a sportswriter. Jumped from a job at *The Montgomery Advertiser* covering Huntingdon College basketball games to the New York Football Giants. I'm loving every day."

"Well, Roll Tide, Bama boy. Don't drink too much and enjoy the party. I gotta go meet someone."

Funny. When she left my side, I thought, who does she remind me of? Ah, of course. Mary Jo Hamilton of high school class reunion fame. See ya, sweetheart.

Then, in she walked. Betty Jean, right on the dot for the kickoff. Gosh, she was beautiful. I rushed to her side and made the unplanned move of kissing her, more like nipping her, on the cheek. She didn't resist, or pull away. She giggled. I took that as a good sign.

I also took her coat, ordered some drinks and a burger, and ushered her to my table. She had been here before, and had friends in the place. She was quickly greeted by a mixed-race married couple, the Andrews, from Brooklyn who always come to Miss Truby's on Saturdays in the Fall. They had found it one day killing time before a Broadway show. They had misread the starting time and couldn't get in the theater that early so they explored the neighborhood. Came across the odd site of a humongous Crimson *A* flag flying on the sidewalk in New York City outside this establishment. They walked in during the second half, ordered food, watched Bama destroy some perennial hapless opponent like Kentucky or somebody, and skipped Broadway. They have come here ever since. They were from Geneva, Alabama. Been here for 15 years, not making a lot in blue-collar type work, but loving it. Even the winters. College football suited their interests much more than *Hello, Dolly* or *Cats*. Besides, folks are confined in a theater. Here you just get up and move freely and you can even use your outside voice if you want to. And here there are very short, if any, lines to the bathrooms, unlike the theater, which are usually only accessible during intermissions. The Andrews were in Bama-transplant heaven.

"What time did you get here?" Betty Jean asked after the Andrews had moved back to their club sandwiches.

"Oh, a bit ago. Didn't want to be late for the big game or the cultural event. I've met several folks, some or all of whom may be friends of yours. Gracious! Lots of Bama blood flowing in this place. I had no idea."

"Just wait! There's a rumor that Joe Namath himself, yep one and the same, Broadway Joe, is going to show up today. May be just a rumor, but we'll see."

I hadn't thought about it till now. But the first time I had met Betty Jean, she told me her daddy had been a coach at Bama when Joe Namath had played there. Daddy had moved to Joe's hometown, Beaver Falls, Pennsylvania, after college before eventually moving back to Bama. That was an original sticking point in my marriage plans, way back in the 8th grade. Funny thing, I could overlook it now. Especially wearing a Bama jacket.

She finally commented on it. She reached across and fingered the Crimson A.

"Nice jacket! What is this I see, Auburn boy? Have you had a life-change, change of heart, or come out of the proverbial college football closet, or what are you doing? Don't tell me you've gone over to the side of the Enemy! The great Crimson Tide of Alabama! Am I gonna hear you say, 'Roll Tide' before the night is over? Hmm?!"

She playfully laughed, and brushed that gorgeous blond hair out of her face while she sipped on her Coke. She had thrown that out there for me to chew on, like fish food on a pond, waiting for the action. I had to respond.

"In all fairness, I didn't buy this…"

"Oh, sure you didn't," she interrupted.

"No, seriously. A guy I don't even know sent it to me. I figured I was coming to a Bama party, might as well dress the part. I didn't want to wear orange and blue and get mugged coming in the front door by some New York City Godfather-like character whose job is to bounce out of here any interlopers. *I come in peace for all Alabama-kind.*"

She smiled, rolled her eyes, shrugged off my attempt at bad humor, and looked at the TV screen. Scoreless, midway through the first quarter. Bama driving.

"There's got to be more to it than that. Wanna try again?"

She was not only drop-dead gorgeous, and perhaps the nicest person I had ever met, but so smart I knew I couldn't keep up. No wonder Emory Doctor Boy left while he was ahead. He wasn't as smart as she was, and he realized it, though he had probably hoped otherwise. He cut his losses and ran.

I murmured to myself that I was different than him. I loved the fact that she was infinitely better looking than me, and much nicer and smarter than I could ever hope to be. I wasn't threatened, nor would I compete with her. I would accept the fact that though I saw her as superior to me, she was God's gift to me, at least at this time in my life, and I would treasure every moment.

I sighed, gathered myself. "Okay, therapist lady, truth be told. It's a long story, and I don't have it sorted out yet, but I challenged myself on the motivation for my college football loyalties. I admit it, feels a little funny. This is the first time I've worn Bama garb in my entire life. But I figured it's time, now that I'm in my 40s, to face reality. With all her faults, I'm proud of my home state. I want the state teams to win. It's good for us! Let's be good at something and attract national attention! George Wallace famously said, 'Thank God for Mississippi or we'd be last in everything!' He was wrong. We are the best at college football. I'm going to cheer for Bama. The Iron Bowl is a separate question. I haven't gotten to that one yet. But I will."

She seemed satisfied. I didn't know how she would take the news. Confessing joint college football loyalties is just not done. Sort of reminded me of the Crimson Tide lady who came to Betty Jean for counseling and revealed her previous engagement to an Auburn man. It was something like a mental health issue. But there was healing for that. Here I was, with mental upheaval over college football allegiance. Was I way off track, or headed towards healing and freedom of spirit? This counselor's brain was no doubt whirring away.

The crowd cheered when Bama scored. And they scored often. Quarterback and eventual MVP Greg McElroy made sure of that. The more they scored, the more profit the brewing companies made. Folks were hugging, laughing, high-fiving, and eventually not even watching. College football is a game. But it is not just a game. It is a platform for fellowship. And this crowd loved them some fellowship.

When the game mercifully ended for the Florida Gators, the crowd had thinned down considerably. Folks had moved on to other venues in the city, with other things to do on a Saturday evening in December. I don't know where Betty Jean got the idea that Joe Namath was coming, but it had indeed just been a rumor. No fact. That was okay. Broadway Joe gave the Bama faithful not just great memories but present-day hope! *He might show up where we are. What?! I'll stick around for that.* I was suspicious from the start that Miss Truby herself, whose photo was on the wall next to Joe, had started the rumor to generate some business. No harm, no foul.

I walked Betty Jean to the door. I wasn't brave enough to try another kiss, albeit a peck on the cheek. But I did grasp her fingers. My heart melted. Especially when she didn't resist.

"See you again?" I asked.

"Definitely," she said. Her eyes darted down momentarily, and she continued, "Joe Billy, things have gotten crazy busy at the homeless shelter, as you might imagine with this growing cold. Lots of hurting people. But I'll find a free slot. Mind if I call you instead of the other way around? I know where we're from it's more proper for the young man to call the young woman, but with my schedule, and I know yours is busy too...I mean call if you want to, but I promise, I'll call when I'm free."

I didn't think that off-course or strange. Any attention from her was fine by me. I said "Great!", followed by "Please do!" My heart leaped within my Bama jacket. Don't know if she noticed or not. Didn't matter. I was right on track for a wonderful future with Bama girl.

I would be sitting by the phone.

25

The Time was 8:46 a.m.

My first New York winter was cold as the mischief. Did I say cold? It snowed, iced, blew, rained, froze, drizzled, and blizzarded. Pretty sure New Yorkers didn't use that word I made up, but I thought it communicated pretty well about what happened when it snowed so hard you could barely walk down the street, you couldn't feel your feet, but if you could you'd swear they were wrapped in ice cubes, and the wind blew so hard it removed toupees and wigs by the dozens. And I wondered: what do the homeless do in this weather? I'm sure they must have figured it out. They were survivors.

The days were short, the nights were long, and work was relentless at *The Post*. The New York Giants had a great season, finishing 12-4. A great season for a new writer. Easy material. Lots of uplifting, winner-like stories. They won their divisional playoff game and their conference championship, smoking the Minnesota Vikings 41-0. We (here I am unconsciously using the first-person plural pronoun; when I plucked it out of my brain, it showed that I had fully made the transition from Bama to New York City), we made it to the Super Bowl! This was a far cry from being at Crampton Bowl, Montgomery, shivering in the December cold at a quickly organized college All-Star game. Not taking anything away from them, but the Super Bowl was the greatest show on earth, and I was there, live and in color. I loved the two weeks of preparation, the in-depth interviews, the game-time reporting and the reflective columns afterward. I wrote some of those about what might have been, as the Giants lost to the Baltimore Ravens. But there was no shame in that. Both had great teams, and the Giants had excelled. I couldn't have asked for a better first year on the job. Pinch me, I'm dreaming.

Usher enjoyed my work and commented with joy on both the negative and positive reviews I got on my columns and reporting. My journalistic skills kept Missy busy answering phone calls from happy and irate customers of *The Post*. It was a New York thing to call and complain. Usher was thrilled that people were reading. He squeezed out a $2,000 raise for me, which I gladly accepted. More than a year in to my new surroundings, I had learned to temper my financial enthusiasm. By the time New York City and Uncle Sam had both taken their shares, there was a little more than I started with, but not enough to fly to the Caribbean, or some such exotic place where you can leave work behind and celebrate accomplishments. Didn't matter. I was happy and fulfilled work-wise. I stayed busy from early to late, doing what I loved. Writing.

However, my big dismal downer was my love life. I never heard from Betty Jean. Despite her promise at the end of the SEC Championship game, on that glorious night at Miss Truby's, "I'll call you, Joe Billy, I promise!", I never heard a word. Thinking that she might have a wrong number, I called her. Weekly. To no avail. She never picked up.

I resolved this dilemma by saying that except for the time growing up together, and casually knowing her, I had lived my life without her. Even when we were in the same school, and I was wonderfully blessed to be in her occasional presence in the same classroom, we did not share a connection. It was only during those three, brief get-togethers that we had experienced anything that approached a meaningful relationship. Oh, well. Glad I kissed her on the cheek when I had the chance.

Maybe reality set in for her, and she knew I was out of my league in trying to get closer to her. I couldn't keep up with Super Woman. Or, maybe an old boyfriend had resurfaced? (Speaking of which, what about Emory Doctor Boy; had he divorced the ER nurse and run back into Betty Jean's arms, with all forgiven and the previous personality analysis no longer valid? He was her hero after all? Fat chance, I said. She's too smart for that.)

All I knew was that time had moved on, and my life had moved on without her. And it was moving pretty fast. I thought of the famous TV line, "As sands through the hour glass, so are the days of our lives." I'll say. The sand was running, and running out quickly. And there was no sight of her. Just a bunch of sand dribbling out, waiting for the blooming gizmo to be turned over and re-initiated. Maybe something good will happen when it starts over.

I had no other love interest. I'll record it in writing without being under duress: I loved Betty Jean Asher. I would have even married her if she had asked *me*. I hope she would have said yes if I had asked her, but who knows? Her disappearance didn't bode well for a positive outcome to my obsession with her. But if I had married her, how would I have ever gotten anything done? All I would want to do is sit and admire her all day. Fancy that. I guess there are worse ways to spend one's life. *Get over her, Joe Billy. Because it's obviously over.*

After the Super Bowl, spring arrived. The boss sent me to cover the Mets and Yankees at their spring training sites in Florida. I loved it. Single guy (albeit an aging single guy) on an expense account in warm climes while NYC was still shivering and stepping in knee-deep puddles filled with ice next to the sidewalks, doing what I loved to do, was fine with me. *The Post* paid all my expenses. I even sub-let my apartment in New York for a few weeks, and made plenty above my rent costs.

I covered the New York Knicks basketball team into the month of May. They were ok, but I wasn't as transfixed to them as I was to the Giants. I was actually glad to see their season end. I couldn't wait for football season to start again.

In July, pro football camps opened, and preseason games followed. I covered my team, the New York Football Giants, and their games, with a passion. In my column, I predicted which players they had drafted who had better improve, or else they would find themselves on the outside looking in, and without a job. I predicted, successfully more than once, which free agent signings were going to the make the 53-man roster, and make a splash in the upcoming National Football League season. I rose to the challenge, writing multiple columns per week. I continued to get kudos from Usher, though I didn't hear as much from him these days. Someone mentioned he had health concerns, or family issues, or something major brewing. I even heard a rumor that he was considering a position offered at *The Baltimore*

Sun. Something about being closer to his dying mother. I didn't know the circumstances, and he didn't talk about them.

I myself was getting a few inquiries from other papers, asking if I would be interested in moving. Editors in Miami and Jacksonville both wrote me multiple times. The editor at the *Kansas City Star* got my cell number somehow and told me I was the answer to their prayers—if I would just accept their offer. They would even pay to move me. I was flattered, but I was staying put for a while longer. Though about as different from Sugar Hill as one could imagine, I experienced what folks were proclaiming about New York City: it grows on you. It won't let you go. You have to forcibly pry its entertaining fingers off you. Besides, I had just been to the Super Bowl! I was ready to go back! These Giants might even be better than last year's outfit. That was an additional strong incentive to stay put.

I was even ready, for the first time since I had moved here, to go back to Bama for a visit. It wasn't cheap to pick up and go, so I needed some advance planning and didn't know how that was going to work out. It was a good time to visit, in the Fall, when Auburn and Alabama were kicking off, and I could see them up close and personal. I would escape from the different and somewhat sterile world of professional football, though I found myself enjoying it more and more. I just needed to get busy and look at some flights to Birmingham. I could finance the trip from my extra rent money I earned from sub-letting my apartment to some newly-landed actor or starving artist who happened to show up during spring training. Life was good, and I was making plans.

On Tuesday, September 11, 2001, I had an appointment at the North Tower of the World Trade Center at 9:00 a.m. Someone I didn't know, who said he was an editor with a book publishing firm, had been reading my columns in *The Post*, liked what he saw, and wondered if I would be interested in some fairly steady, freelance work editing new manuscripts. From his brief description on the phone, I wasn't sure with my work load that I could manage it, but I told him I would come down for a chat. I wasn't due in the office until noon that day. Maybe if things went well, and we extended the chat, the editor would offer to buy me early lunch at the Observation Deck? That would be a treat. I didn't get to the WTC very often.

Instead of the Local train I was expecting and which often took even longer due to the constant NYC announcements, "The New York Transit Authority will be working on the tracks this week on such and such a line between such and such a stop", I was able to get an Express, and I got to the building about 30 minutes early. I figured with the anticipated train schedule, I would have probably gotten to the lobby about 8:45, but arriving at 8:30 was a bonus. Nice to have a few brief minutes of white space.

After going through the sign-ins and security checks and all that goes with a major office building, I went over and pushed an up-elevator button. And waited. Lots of beeps and lights indicating where the elevators were, but none of them were moving towards the lobby. At least not quickly.

While I kept staring at the lights above the elevators, and keeping track of their progress, and noting that one was on the tenth floor and finally moving my way, my cell phone rang. I didn't recognize the number, but it was an Alabama area code, so I took it. It was an incoming call from someone I hadn't talked to in years.

"Joe Billy? Paul Washington!"

"Are you kidding me? Paul, how are you? Where are you?"

"I'm in Birmingham. Just had a job change. Believe it or not, I'm managing the Galleria Mall in Hoover. It's a new start, and so far, so good. Hey, have you got a minute?"

I was thrilled to hear from this old friend. I told him I didn't have long, but would love to catch up with him. I actually couldn't hear him too well in the spot where I was standing, and trying to connect from the elevator, which finally arrived in front of me, would be without success. I told him to hold on a minute. I would change locations. I knew of a small diner less than two blocks away. I would go there and take the call, and wait for my appointment time, especially since I was early and had a little cushion. Besides, I could use a little caffeine. He mumbled okay and hung up.

I got to the diner about 8:35. I called him back.

"Joe Billy, I'm actually headed to Sugar Hill this afternoon. Going home to visit my mom who's not well."

"I'm sorry, Paul. What's the problem?"

And on it went, family news, and some chit chat and catching up. Then he got to the point.

"I've got two tickets for Saturday's Bama-Southern Miss game at Legion Field in Birmingham. I know you're an Auburn guy, but being a big fancy sportswriter in the Big Apple, I wanted to make sure you had a chance to remember what real football is like. I've actually got a business proposition for you as a side conversation. Maybe after the game we could do dinner and talk more. I'm buying."

It all sounded good. And I could explain the Auburn metamorphosis thing I had been through when I saw him. Maybe. If I needed to.

I looked at my watch. I had better get moving. It was 8:44.

"Paul, I need to get to an appointment. I've been wanting to come home for a visit. This sounds like as good an excuse as any. Can we talk later today?"

"Definitely. I'm here. I'll be whipping the Galleria in shape all day. Call me! Bye."

At 8:45 Paul hung up the phone. I stepped outside the diner in a hurry, in a rush to cover the two blocks back to the WTC, as I didn't want to be late, especially after having arrived early. That always irritated me: getting within striking distance of a place ahead of schedule, but not actually getting to the place until after the appointed time, distracted by some sidebar idea that seemed good at the time.

I had taken less than six steps on the sidewalk when I heard a deafening boom. *What was that?!*

I instinctively looked in the direction of the noise, and I saw the oddest thing: an airplane, marked by American Airlines signage, sticking in the side of the North Tower of the World Trade Center. Thick, black smoke was billowing, emanating from the point of impact. I could see fire. My brain was trying its best to process what I was seeing. But I made no sense of it.

I was paralyzed. With confusion. And with fright. *What's happening?*

I wasn't too aware of my surroundings, but I do recall that people all along this street where I was standing were running out of their shops and cafes and pointing and screaming and trying to understand what had just happened. Mostly, like me, they were in shock. There is no word in English to describe this level of disbelief or the failure to grasp the meaning of what we were seeing.

I know what I was thinking. "Man, that pilot really goofed up! Was he headed to LaGuardia, or JFK, and lost control? Was he leaving LaGuardia and got lost, maybe had a heart attack in the cockpit? This is unbelievable!"

As the smoke increased, and flames grew higher, I inched my way forward for a better look. People started stumbling past me, away from the WTC. They were running for their lives, with terror etched on their faces. Mothers were pushing strollers as fast as they could stand it. They were weeping, horrified.

I heard sirens. The New York Fire Department was careening through the streets. The NYPD was on the way. Ambulances were appearing from everywhere.

The closer I got, the louder were the screams. Then the building started collapsing.

Who knows how long it was that I stood and stared. I do know I was there long enough to witness folks finding holes in the building and jumping. From 30, 40, 50 stories. I could only imagine that they were thinking that if they stayed inside, they would burn to death. If they jumped, maybe someone, somehow, would catch them, or help them break their fall, or the Fire Department would position a catcher for them to fall into. That gave them, I reasoned, at least a hope of survival. Inside the building, their chances appeared to be zero. The Fire Department was on the way, but this was probably going to be a rescue operation rather than a fire extinguishing exercise. The building was not going to stay intact.

I pulled out my phone and called the office. I wanted to know if anyone had the story. But I couldn't get through. The lines were jammed.

I tried again. Nothing. A third time. The same.

While some of the spectators got closer to the scene and wondered what we could possibly do to help in our paralyzed state, overwhelmed by the sheer magnitude of this disaster, the unthinkable happened. A United Airlines jet hit the South Tower at 9:03 a.m.

Same result. Duplicate chaos. But a different conclusion: this was not pilot error. This was intentional. New York City's air space had been invaded and violated. Within sight of the Statue of Liberty, our nation's freedom was under attack.

Now what?

26

The Aftermath

Life changed forever for me on 9/11. I was never the same.

The context of my life had revolved around sports, and specifically football, for as long as I could remember. But now, it didn't seem so important. Our city had changed, along with our country, and our world. Recreation and entertainment and team loyalties dropped way down the list of things I was interested in. I was a numb New Yorker for months afterwards.

I kept writing for *The Post* but I was a changed man. Howard Usher had died in his office due to heart failure late one afternoon. His passing also added to my gloom. I had grown fond of him. Management asked me to step into a senior sports writer role, and my love for my profession increased even more with new, daily reporting challenges, new entrances into the leadership of the newspaper, and a new salary, which helped me to cope with continuing NYC price increases. I regularly spurned offers from other papers. I found it flattering to be courted and wanted by others. But I could land no good reason to leave New York. It had grabbed me, grown on me, and wouldn't dare let go.

I made firms plans to go back to Sugar Hill for a visit, but definitely not on the weekend that Paul Washington called me. And not just because college football games were cancelled, and flights were cancelled, and the world was in general chaos. But because life was spinning, and I needed to stay in New York for a while to try to regain some balance, and find a place of resilience. I wanted to help my fellow New Yorkers recover, but I wasn't sure how. I participated in food drives and blood drives, and helped those who were assisting the police and fire departments in their work and in their grieving. But I'm sure I didn't make much of an impact. Maybe it was for me more than them; so many of us just wanted to help, wanted to do something, but we didn't really know how. At least we tried.

I hadn't been to Sugar Hill since my class reunion. On arrival, about nine months after 9/11, I was struck by the imagery that the streets, houses, and shops looked mostly the same as it had during my youth. As I walked the streets, I found City Barber. I went inside, and chatted for a bit, though not recognizing anyone. I learned that Mr. Ronnie, my barber, had died last year, dramatically experiencing a heart attack in the middle of a crewcut. He had been replaced by a young, smiley fellow who had noticeably raised the rates and spruced the place up a bit inside. I learned that Mr. Leroy had retired and moved to Mobile to be near his grandchildren. I exited and went by the Methodist Church. Needing a bit of paint, but it was the same. And so, my tour of town continued. Not much purpose, but a try at getting re-acquainted with what I had known in my childhood.

Somewhere in the first day of the visit, I realized that underneath, things were different from what I had known. The town looked the same, but I had changed. I was a New Yorker now, and had lost my small-town edge. For the first time in my life, I felt that I was a visitor to Sugar Hill. It was no longer home. I was ready to return to 88th and

Amsterdam to what was now familiar. It would be a relief to get back home.

As the aftermath of 9/11 unfolded, as with all New Yorkers, I tried to make sense of what I had witnessed. The over-arching question was why? Why would someone do this? Were they mad, as in angry mad, or mad, as in insanely mad, or both?

As the investigation continued, and the facts were uncovered, and plotters interrogated, I was not at all surprised that this horror was linked back to racial and religious prejudice. The scourge of the world, ancient and modern, was still in play. Among other reasons for their senseless act, the Islamic terrorists openly declared their disdain for the United States of America in light of our support and help and alliance with the Jewish state of Israel.

"I'll attack you because of who you are, and what you stand for. You think differently from me, and you have different friends who are of a different religion. They are of Isaac, and we are of Ishmael. Never mind that you are not attacking me, at least not directly. I will attack you, for you align yourselves with Isaac.

"And I will do so because I have been carefully taught to hate."

In the aftermath of this tragedy, as I tried to make sense of the new world we were living in and the overt hatred of self-proclaimed enemies, I did the smart thing: I underwent therapy, both in individualized and in group sessions. Some humor helped, and I almost chuckled when I thought of the irony: *I'm a real New Yorker now! I'm in therapy!* As Betty Jean had once told me, she never knew anyone in Sugar Hill who was a therapist. Not that they weren't needed. They just weren't present. But they were in New York, and I sought them out. I'm glad I did.

I needed help. I had witnessed both planes hitting the towers. I dreamed about it. Never went a day without thinking about it. If I pondered long enough, I could see people jumping. I could hear the screams, smell the smoke, almost feel the rush of wind with fire trucks whizzing past me. I could see both towers collapsing as I stood on that sidewalk in disbelief. Those thoughts and images stayed with me for years. Unlike the images stored in my brain of Jobab Robinson flying down the field, or Bo Jackson going over the top, or Bear Bryant in houndstooth fedora leaning against a goal post at Legion Field in pre-game warmups. I could dial those up if needed. But the 9/11 images surfaced, whether I wanted them to or not. And they often surfaced when I didn't want them to. Like in the middle of the night when I desperately wanted sleep.

The thing that kept me up at night was one key reality that I had suppressed. It had been there all along, lurking beneath my willingness to deal with it. It only came out in therapy when I found the courage to face survivor's guilt and admit the horrifying truth: *I was supposed to be in that North Tower.* If either the elevator had been quicker, or Paul Washington hadn't called, I would have been.

To confront this demon even more boldly, I eventually got access to a floor plan of the North Tower. I scoped out the location of the office of the publishing house editor who had invited me for a chat on the morning of September 11. I became nauseous upon realizing it was on the same side of the building, two floors below where the American Airlines jet had struck. I researched further and discovered the editor's name as one of the 3,000 or so who died that day. May he rest in peace. God bless his family.

In my therapy sessions, I also dealt with prejudice, and significantly, my thoughts towards the plane hijackers and master-mind attackers who had been discovered to be motivated by the USA's alliance with Israel. Pulling out of me what I really thought about those evil people was not easy. But once it started coming out, I didn't hold back. It wasn't pretty. Week after week in those sessions, though, I felt more alive. Though extremely painful, I deduced it was because I was becoming more honest with myself, and I was facing reality rather than suppression of thoughts. I was on the way to healing.

I admit that in counseling I expressed my disdain, and at times what manifested as hatred, for those who attacked our country, and who killed innocent thousands on that day—hundreds of whom were immigrants to the United States, working in the financial capital of the world. It was good to be guided by a trained professional and move towards the removal of my debilitating thoughts which I was harboring—and which to be honest, I had not expressed until I received counseling.

As I've mentioned in my memoir, racial prejudice was part of the fabric of Alabama society in my youth, and even more so in the lives of my parents. Therapy helped me to address the issue: what were signs of prejudice in my life? We had dealt extensively with the terrorists and their obvious prejudices and unspeakably horrible behaviors. But I wanted to know what was inside of *me*, and deal with it, before it led to destructive behavior. I couldn't actually think of any prejudices I was holding, nor was I exhibiting any signs of racism. But as I looked back on my life, I became aware that humans are given to blind spots. I sought help to see if I had some that were unnoticed, and which should be unwelcomed.

I wondered about other real or potential prejudices in my life, apart from racism. What about prejudice—perhaps brought on by confusion, or was it hardness of heart?—towards the homeless, which the reader of my memoir has encountered on more than one page. I wondered about various types of people, and their shapes and sizes and attitudes and political affiliations. Did I demonstrate unhealthy—and often unrealized—prejudice towards them?

I even wondered about a defining characteristic of my life, which has been evident in these pages: namely, unending and fully expressed loyalties for sports teams. The bond we form with fellow fans of our team, or teams, is a beautiful thing. I came to the helpful discovery in therapy that for the most part, team loyalties and affections are a demonstrated *preference*, rather than a *prejudice*. Those two are not the same.

We live with preferences, and in fact, our life revolves around them. Whether it be choices between chocolate and vanilla, or steak and chicken, the kinds of books we read, movies we watch or music we listen to, whether we like to have clean-shaven faces or full beards, and of course, which college football teams we follow and live and die with.

Preferences are personal. Sometimes they go way over the top, as demonstrated by my dad's brother, Uncle Moon Pie. Reflecting on his hyper-preference for his team of choice, I give him extra points for passion, which is an element of preference.

Prejudice is also personal, but with a key difference, and this also came out in my therapy sessions: prejudice crosses from the realm of simple, personal choice and preference to destructive behavior towards others. Those actions cannot be justified as legitimate or acceptable. Preferences can be justified, however, and we cannot fault others for those. That's part of how they are built, no matter the process behind that building of self and identity.

I think of Jobab Robinson. He didn't spurn the University of Alabama and choose the University of the South because he was prejudiced against the Tide; he preferred the academic program at Sewanee. He also preferred not to interject himself into the racially tenuous world of college football in the South in the second half of the 20th century. From my perspective, he followed his heart, and that was a healthy choice.

We often rejoice in our choices of preference, we nurture them, we gather and celebrate with those who enjoy the same ones, and we receive satisfaction in how they bring us repeated pleasure! *Long live our preferences!* But as I have learned, we are in deep trouble if we rejoice in our prejudices.

It takes a long time to get to the bottom of our hearts. I regret that 9/11 was the catalyst for that period of discovery in my life. I'm definitely healthier because of those self-discoveries, but the circumstances for achieving that position of increased health and wholeness will hopefully never be repeated.

I have taken comfort in the fact that hate does not win in the end, even though sometimes it feels so strong that one would think it's invincible.

It's not.

God's love will triumph. And in this I am comforted.

27

The Most-Awkward Surprise

I mentioned previously that Betty Jean never called, and I was never able to contact her, though I tried repeatedly, without success. Just as well. When 9/11 occurred, I became so numb and overwhelmed from what I had witnessed at the World Trade Center, I found it easy to shrug and move on from the thoughts of courtship. Life didn't make sense. My numbness towards Betty Jean was one more piece of evidence attesting to my continuing detachment from the normal feelings I had known. She was out of sight, and for the most part, out of mind, as a whole list of things were that had previously featured prominently in my thoughts.

That is, until, once again, she resurfaced.

I was in my favorite store in New York, The M&M Store, at Times Square. I liked to go there occasionally to browse the new merchandise reflective of my favorite candy, and also to stock up for my sweet tooth, doing so with a personalized flair.

I was standing off to the side near the escalator on the bottom floor one Saturday afternoon. I just happened to look up and a little tyke, three or four years old, came bursting through the front door squealing, adorned in a Crimson Tide sweatshirt, of all things. Just behind him was a man that I assumed was his daddy. He was a big, handsome guy. He picked up Little Man and pointed across the store and I heard him say, "Who's that?"

Little Man screamed and laughed, and without saying a word, ran as fast as he could through the M&M treasures, right into the arms of a beautiful blonde, no more than 15 feet from me.

Betty Jean Asher. Unmistakably her.

She scooped him up, stroked his hair, grabbed his cheeks in a playful sort of way, and grinned from ear to ear. She cuddled him and cooed over him. Obviously knew him quite well.

Of course, I was shocked. Without a word, nor an approach to her, I stopped whatever browsing I was doing, and turned to hurry out the door that Big Handsome Guy had just walked through. My mind was churning. And immediately conclusive. That's why Betty Jean had never called me: she was married to Big Handsome Guy, and this bundle of locomotive energy squealing around the M&M gift bins was their son. Good for them, but I couldn't face their reality. I had been through enough reality to know that I didn't want any more.

I took about three hurried steps, darting towards the exit, and I heard her voice: "Joe Billy?!" Those were the same words she had uttered in the same way in our chance encounter at Five Napkin Burger on a night that now seemed like another lifetime ago.

I cringed. I knew I was trapped, and there was no way to sidestep this embarrassing situation. I would have to face her.

It was a similar feeling to what I had experienced during our class reunion when Mary Jo Hamilton had thrown herself at me. I couldn't wriggle out of interacting with Mary Jo, but I could cut it short and disappear. I had also used the clear-signal approach of "not interested", and that had worked decisively well.

But with Betty Jean, it was different. It's not that I didn't want to talk to her. I was actually relieved that the long hunt was over. I had found her. Reflecting again on our communication silence, I had sat by the phone for so long, waiting for her to call, I had given up ever seeing her again. I had imagined that in my efforts to contact her I must have had the wrong number, or she had changed phones without telling me (and maybe I wasn't in her new address book?!). I remember that for a long time after that night at Miss Truby's, I almost jumped every time the phone rang. Maybe it was her! I could not bring myself to conclude that she was just ignoring me. She had shown what I had felt was genuine interest in at least getting together again. Her silence did not make sense.

But for all my mental backtracking as to why we had not connected, or if I had done something wrong which I had not been aware of, the reason was now clear, and he was standing just behind me. All vain excuses were shoved to the side and categorized as a bad, drawn-out memory. I had prided myself on having been able to work through the fatal tragedy of losing my fiancé-to-be, Susan B. Anthony. But it didn't take much soul-searching to discover the obvious: I had never gotten over Betty Jean.

I was now in her presence. And I had to respond.

Unless I just blew by her and headed for the door, I would have to be polite, take it like a man, and be introduced to the one who had won her heart. I would meet the man who had done what I had not been able to do. Mr. Right, Mr.

Lucky, or whoever he was, had something I didn't. I would have to confess that it was "game over."

I had no choice but to stop and turn, and face the one who called out my name. My surreptitious great escape was foiled, and we were now in each other's presence, locking eyes in what for me was an extremely awkward moment. I would be remiss if I didn't add that her eyes were just as beautiful as I remembered them. However, my feeling of awkwardness was immeasurable. I would have been very happy for the earth to swallow me whole and then close on top of me, thus alleviating the need to inform me why she had never followed through on her promise to call me. I now had the reason, and what was left to discuss? Besides, I had crawled out of the hole in my life that was opened by 9/11. I would resist any possibility of going back inside that dark place, even temporarily.

As we stood in each other's presence, my face flushed hot. Hers seemed to glow red just for a second, but I wasn't sure if that was her skin, or if my eyes were going into over-drive and playing tricks on me. I do recall that I was experiencing what we referred to as kids as "cotton-mouth", and I was aware that it would be hard to successfully form words that were clear and distinct.

I was aware that my breathing was shallow. I was embarrassed, speechless, and insecure. Not exactly the masculine *persona* I wished to portray in the presence of the nicest and most beautiful female I had ever known. I would have to immediately invent a false front, and appear cool, relaxed, and delighted.

My mental fumbling about what to say and how to start a meaningful dialogue suddenly didn't matter. She spoke first.

"Joe Billy, it's really you! I didn't know if I would ever see you again. Let me introduce you to my brother Calvin, and his son, Nick."

28

The Explanation

Betty Jean said she was stunned to see *me*? As Old Man Parker had no doubt uttered on numerous occasions around the poker table, I'll see yours, and raise you two.

I exchanged greetings with her brother and playful nephew, and we abandoned our shopping trip and left, trying to find a place to talk. Never easy in the Times Square area, but we managed. I don't remember where we went besides it being some little café that actually had an open table in the back. There, Betty Jean laid out for me a story full of twists and turns, reminiscent of Alabama country roads. Where was this leading? Most of the time in her story, I could not see at all around the corner. And there were no straightaways to catch my breath.

She dropped the news that not long after that memorable night at Miss Truby's, it was discovered that she had contracted breast cancer. Her world, of course, shattered and went into a spin. She had faced it alone, and she described the deep darkness in which she lived. Every day, she wondered if it would be her last. She spoke at some length of her double mastectomy, and the ensuing radiation, and the effects on her physically, mentally and emotionally. As a professional counselor, she was clear in her presentation. She was steady and balanced as she shared with me her steps to healing. I hung on every word. I felt that I had entered fully into her life-changing dilemma, and in some odd way, that I had been there with her throughout the ordeal.

Then she introduced the next chapter of family tragedy, handing the floor over to her brother Calvin. Through tears, and with wounds still fresh, he cleared his throat and told how his wife Sarah had died in the South Tower on 9/11. They had moved to New York for him to work for Deloitte in a job he couldn't turn down. Sarah had already become an accomplished pediatrician, and was excited about their relocation from Pittsburgh, eager to take on the challenge of practicing medicine in the USA's largest city. She was actually off work on September 11, and had gone to the WTC to run an errand, delivering a small gift to a friend from high school that she discovered had recently moved to The City, and who was in her office on that fateful morning. Calvin's recounting of his grief over his loss of wife left me speechless.

At the time of Sarah's death, baby Nick was several months old. Calvin needed help, and Betty Jean offered to take a sabbatical from her counseling ministry with the homeless to help raise the little guy and be his nanny. Brother and sister grew exceptionally close. Shared tragedy has a way of doing that.

But there was more. Betty Jean recounted how 18 months after the Towers fell, their mom Lucy was diagnosed with esophageal cancer. Betty Jean had scoured the Internet and located our classmate, Dr. Jobab Robinson, whose star was continuing to rise in the world of cancer research. They talked several times, and he suggested options for treatment, meds, and therapy, all of which were instrumental in Lucy's eventual healing. But it was a long, exhausting road to that point. Betty Jean's father had died some time ago, and she and Calvin were left to care for mom. The bulk of the duty fell to Betty Jean, and she made many trips to Pennsylvania, with Nick in tow, to attend to Lucy. But Lucy was now okay, and had re-entered a mostly normal life, surrounded by friends and ongoing medical care.

I was spellbound, listening to their story. I had never known anyone who had been through such layers of pain and upheaval. But they had survived. And it was obvious to this observer that they had come out stronger.

By its nature, a memoir is a perfect place to recount valuable life lessons, even those that are a bit embarrassing to admit. Here's one from that day: *the world doesn't revolve around me.* I took it personally that Betty Jean had not called. But on reflection of her now-revealed journey, I remembered the popular song of Carly Simon from the 1970s, "You're so vain. You probably think this song is about you, don't you?! You're so vain."

Though Betty Jean had often filled my thoughts since our chance encounter a couple of years before, of course I had not been aware that her life had morphed into a nightmare of successive challenges. Her focus had been reduced to just a few, repeating, lasered points of attention. I was ashamed when I thought her silence was all about me. I had succumbed to my vanity.

I also regretted that I had not been there to help. But as I listened and quietly rejoiced in the hard-fought healing to which they had arrived, I was honest with myself that I had not been needed. I would like to think I could have helped, being a friend who could give and not expect anything in return. However, it is possible that the drama that inevitably comes with any new, dating relationship would have just complicated things. Trying to manage that in the midst of what they were going through might have led to heartbreak. And really, did they need one more thing to deal with? It was actually for the best that I had not been in the picture. They were the ones to handle it, and had obviously passed the test.

Remarkable people.

Epilogue

Two years later, I married my eighth-grade crush in a glorious ceremony filled with crimson and white, and orange and blue. Not even the M&Ms at the reception escaped the color parade.

Calvin stood beside me as my best man. Paul Washington was next to Calvin, and my boyhood friend Jimmy Hightower was also there in the groomsmen lineup. Jobab Robinson sent his regrets. He was fully involved at Oxford in a clinical trial of a potential game-changing cancer drug.

The wedding ceremony went off without a hitch. For one thing, the timing was perfect, making the wedding planner absolutely giddy. The date was the last Saturday in June, two months before the earliest college football kickoff, and two months after the Bama spring game. At Bryant-Denny, it's not unusual to have 92,000 show up for that event to see the talent they can look forward to in the fall. So, in deference to that annual ritual, bypassing a late April wedding date was imperative. As a bonus, this wonderful timing wiped out the possibility of interference from a suddenly unplugged, tucked-away transistor radio tuned to the Auburn game.

With shouts of joy, and feasting, and smiles all around, Betty Jean and I were now a House United.

I wondered if ours were the first marriage vows with the proclamations of *Roll Tide!* and *War Eagle!* uttered in the same ceremony.

Acknowledgements

My family has been full of encouragement through this entire writing venture. My wife Bekah has been an active cheerleader, urging me to pursue my dream of story-telling over the last 20 years that this story has been percolating. She, along with my son John, and his wife, Lauren; my son David, and his wife, Jasmine; and my daughter Kathryn, all listened to audio readings of earlier drafts and made invaluable comments with critical insights. Thank you! Y'all are wonderful.

I acknowledge with appreciation my school teachers, from grades 1-12, who taught me to read, write and think. Where would I be in life without the privilege of their patient instruction?

Speaking of which, three college and graduate school professors urged me on in advanced ways to hone a craft for writing. David Ringer first introduced me to the logistical complexity of developing a novel. Those comments planted a seed. He also tirelessly worked with me to improve my writing skills. Robert Tuttle made a comment on a term paper that impacted me: "You have a gift for writing. Pursue this gift." Robert Mansfield instructed me on the art of rewriting through a painful, yet rewarding, master's thesis process. Thank you, gentlemen.

I am indebted to the writing coach I hired for feedback on this project, Mark Malatesta. His insights shaped and reshaped my approach, opening my eyes to target audience considerations and plot development.

Alan and E'Lynne Elliot and Patsey Summey helped to start the Dallas Area Writer's Group in Cedar Hill, Texas, of which I was an early participant. Their enthusiasm, personal support, and quest for learning and writing improvement were a gift to me. Thanks, y'all.

John Grisham played a vicarious role in this production. (No, I don't personally know John, but would love the opportunity to have lunch.) I was struck by the author's note at the beginning of *A Time to Kill*, in which he wrote:

> My goal when I began writing this book was simply to complete it. I could envision a neat pile of typed pages over in the corner of my office, and one day I would be able to point to it with some measure of pride and explain to clients and friends that it was a novel I had written. Surely, somewhere in the deep recesses of my mind, I dreamed of getting it published, but I honestly can't remember such thoughts, at least not when I started writing. It would become my first prolonged effort at fiction.

He went on to detail the writing process, and the sixteen agents and twelve publishers who passed on it, and how he was finally able to find an agent for it. (That's what I have been unable to do for this book; and that's ok. I'm in good company, it seems, and maybe I just gave up too soon!) Grisham went on to say that:

It was a first novel, and most of them are ignored.
[And I wryly add: "We can't all be Harper Lee."]
Better things were just around the corner.

He concluded by saying,

This one came from the heart. It's a first novel, and
at times it rambles, but I wouldn't change a word if
given the chance.

I hear you, John.
Amen.